AND ALL THE RIVERS BETWEEN

GLENDA GILLASPY

ISBN 978-1-64079-122-0 (Paperback)
ISBN 978-1-64079-124-4 (Hard Cover)
ISBN 978-1-64079-123-7 (Digital)

Copyright © 2017 by Glenda Gillaspy
All rights reserved. No part of this publication may be reproduced, distributed, or transmitted in any form or by any means, including photocopying, recording, or other electronic or mechanical methods without the prior written permission of the publisher. For permission requests, solicit the publisher via the address below.

Christian Faith Publishing, Inc.
296 Chestnut Street
Meadville, PA 16335
www.christianfaithpublishing.com

Printed in the United States of America

This book is dedicated to my husband, my family, and friends who have cheered me on as I wrote it. I am especially grateful to my niece, Jeana, without whose help and encouragement, I would have never completed it. I love you all.

PROLOGUE

THE VALLEY GLOWED WITH PINK and purple as the deep red sun slowly sank behind the mountain in the distance. The river below sang a pleasant watery song as it meandered on down the valley. It brought to mind a poem she had written for Lonnie years ago as they left home and family to set off on their adventure on the wagon train.

AND ALL THE RIVERS BETWEEN

Under the stars on a dark summer's night
my love and I would dream our dreams,
of traveling to far off places of delight
such pleasure did it seem.
Under the stars on a dark summer's night
we'd talk of all we'd see;
of the mighty river we're leaving now
and all the rivers between.

Yes, from the mighty Mississippi
to Oregon's beauty supreme,
till we cross the Jordan at Heaven's gate
and all the rivers between.

ELAINE PUSHED A STRAY WISP of gray hair from her face as she watched a hawk circling the meadow, searching for a careless field mouse. Elaine Denton Ross had been an eyeful in her youth by anyone's standards—all of five feet tall with her shoes on, tiny and petite. Fiery red hair had framed her heart-shaped face. She had always hated her hair, having taken much teasing over it as a child. Her large, hazel eyes were truly the window to her soul. Nanny always said, "Ain't no ust you tryin' ta lie ta me, Little Missy, 'cuz yo eyes done giz you away, an' dat's a fac'!" The lashes that framed those eyes were like thick copper-colored brushes that delicately swept her cheeks each time she blinked. Nanny was the old Negress who had raised her from an infant. Elaine had loved that old black woman who had been more of a mother to her than her own mother had been.

Time, wind, and sun had taken its toll on her once beautiful creamy skin, giving it a leathery look. Lines were deeply etched into her face, perky freckles giving way to blotches.

Lizzie B stepped out onto the porch tying her sunbonnet. She leaned down to place her smooth cheek next to her mother's parched one. "Are you going to be all right, Mama? Why don't I leave Charla here with you tonight? Is that okay with you?"

"Yes, honey, That'll be fine. Charla and I will keep each other company," she answered with a smile.

"Ellen told her to stay the night with us, but I knew as soon as she got over here with her Nanaw that her Grammy would take second place!" She grinned. "I'll see you tomorrow then." Lizzie B. kissed her mother then stooped down to eye level with her seven-year-old granddaughter. "You be good now, sweetie, and your mama or I will be back to get you tomorrow. Take good care of Nanaw."

"I will, Grammy," Charla answered with a hug. They watched as Lizzie B. drove away, the buggy kicking up a cloud of dust behind each wheel.

"Look what I'm making for you!" The child held up her embroidery hoop and showed the colorful flowers stitched onto the handkerchief it held.

Elaine looked to see the offered gift. "Your stitching is getting so much nicer, Charla." She smoothed the blond curls softly with a gnarled, blemished hand. "I shall carry it right here in my pocket."

Dimples leapt into view as the little girl smiled up at her great-grandmother.

"Why don't we go into the house, Honey. You'll ruin your eyes trying to stich out here in this low light." Elaine laboriously stood up, holding to the porch railing momentarily to get her balance. She took Charla by the hand and led her inside. Lighting the lamps as she moved through the house, soon a comforting golden glow bathed the room. "Are you hungry, dear?" she asked.

"Not very, but I would like some of your good sugar cookies." The child looked up hopefully at Nanaw.

Elaine frowned. "Your mama would skin me alive if she knew I was letting you eat sugar cookies for supper!" She hesitated for a moment then continued with a grin. "Oh, well, I guess it won't hurt anything this one time, if you'll drink a big glass of milk with them."

"I promise!"

They went into the kitchen and Charla crawled up into one of the heavy wooden chairs that Papaw had made with his own hands. They were worn with time but still sturdy. She watched as Nanaw got the cookie jar and placed two large sugar cookies on a plate and set a glass of milk down in front of her. "Thank you, Nanaw," she said sweetly.

"You're welcome, honey," Elaine replied.

Charla thought Nanaw looked very sad tonight, making her look older somehow. "Nanaw, how old are you?" she asked, inquisitive as most seven-year-olds are.

"Well, Miss Impertinence, it's not polite to ask a lady her age but since it's you, I'll tell you," teased Nanaw. "I'm seventy-five."

"Seventy-five!" breathed Charla.

"That's right! I was born in 1832 in a place called St. Louis, Missouri." Nanaw smiled down at Charla. "Yes, ma'am! I've certainly seen a lot of changes in this old world from then to now. I still can't get used to saying "1907"! The "nineteen" part still throws me."

Charla giggled. "I've seen Missouri on a map in school and it *is* a long way off!" Charla said, very impressed. "Please, Nanaw, tell me more! Did you have any brothers or sisters?"

"No, it was just me!" replied Nanaw, smiling.

"What games did you play when you were little? Did you know Papaw when he was a little boy? What did your house look like?" Charla stopped to take a breath.

Nanaw held up her hand. "Whoa, there! You're asking a lot of questions! Are you sure you feel like hearing a story that long?"

"Oh, yes, ma'am, I want to hear all about it. Please tell me!"

"Finish your cookies and milk then we'll go into the parlor so we can be comfortable and I'll tell you."

Elaine opened a trunk that sat at the foot of her bed. She moved a lamp closer so she could see the items kept there. Her hands caressed each thing they touched, as though they were priceless jewels. Then she found what she had been looking for; a book, but not just any book. It was her journal, lovingly kept since she was a girl back in St. Louis. She closed her eyes, still smiling slightly as memories came flooding back. She carried it back to the parlor, placing the lamp on the table beside the sofa.

Charla crawled up into her lap. "I'm ready now, Nanaw. I ate my cookies and drank every drop of my milk!" she said proudly, yawning in spite of herself.

"Good for you!" Nanaw gave her a big hug. She opened the journal and lovingly turned the pages. It had been almost three quarters of a century since she had been the girl she could see in her mind, but in some ways it seemed like only yesterday. She could almost smell Imogene's fresh bread baking in the kitchen and hear the sounds of the carriages in the city.

CHAPTER 1

St. Louis, Missouri, teemed with life in 1850. The city, though raw, held beauty and excitement, and above all, an air of expectancy! Dreams came true in this place! New money and old money flowed through this crossroads city as she writhed with growing pains.

From the time Missouri had achieved statehood in 1820, traffic had steadily increased. The city quickly became the "jumping off" place for those adventurous souls who were on their way west to find their fortunes. Those fortunes took many shapes; homesteads for some, and fur trading for others. Some were on their way just to be going, with no particular goal in mind. They seemed to be following some invisible hand that beckoned to them from the west.

The joining of the two largest rivers in the country made St. Louis a veritable melting pot of cultures, lifestyles, and ideologies. The population doubled from 1840 to 1850, making her a major metropolis with almost eighty thousand residents. River travel was largely responsible. The streets teemed with masses of people as the city continued to grow by leaps and bounds. A hodgepodge of French, Spanish, English, and American architecture adorned her bluffs and valleys.

The fur trade, and the support businesses it generated, produced big money for lots of people. They were from all walks of life. There were the well-bred, well-educated folk, proud of their heritage and determined to continue the traditions and culture of the diverse places from which they had come.

Many of the "newly rich" were uneducated and unrefined; untrained in the social graces of the civilized world. Some of these folk were preposterous, fawning social climbers, steeped in flashy vulgarity, flaunting their wealth at every opportunity. They desperately wanted the acceptance of the old genteel families of the community. The new elite and the old genteel did meet occasionally at the various social functions, but a definite invisible line divided the two groups.

On the bluffs overlooking the city stood the homes of the well-to-do. In a prestigious two-and-a-half-story brick mansion lived the Denton family. Ralph Denton's father had settled in St. Louis, moving from Kentucky in the late 1700s. Their family was considered to be part of the real gentility in the city. Ralph married the beautiful Blanche Renault from an old New Orleans family and built her this house in 1831. Lovely Victorian pillars supported a spacious veranda on the second floor. A grand iron fence surrounded the yard, like sentinels guarding the mansion. A massive gate, beautiful with intricate ornate iron work, gave entry to the grounds.

Elaine was a precocious child, giving Nanny much exasperation and trying her caregiver's patience more times than could be counted. She thought Nanny looked even blacker when she was angry because her eyes got so big you could see the whites against her black skin! But at night, Nanny would pull her up on her ample lap and sing to the little girl she loved so much. Elaine learned about Jesus there on Nanny's lap. She made Him sound so wonderful, and she talked to Him like He was right there in the room with them! Elaine wished she could see Him too. Nanny said someday she would. After she fell asleep, Nanny would gently tuck her into the beautiful canopy bed and blow out the lamp. Elaine thought no little girl in the world could have been as lucky as she!

Elaine's thoughts came back to the present. She looked down at Charla, sleeping like an angel beside her on the couch, and smiled. Tenderly, she covered her up and kissed her forehead. "Good night, little one," she whispered. She took the journal and the lamp into the bedroom and settled down for an evening of reminiscence.

As a child, Elaine played with the slave children under the lilac bushes and the big oak trees that shaded their yard. Papa had instructed Ramsey, their groundskeeper, to build a swing on the big oak in the back yard. It had an inviting limb that protruded from the trunk at a ninety degree angle, looking as though it was just waiting for a rope for children to play on. The youngsters, black and white, would play for hours. Elaine would let the black children swing when she grew tired. In those days, even the very young knew the boundaries between black and white, and slave children would never have dreamed of trying to take a turn on the swing as long as "Little Missy" wanted it.

Imogene's daughter, Trixie, and Elaine were best friends back then. Trixie, a light-skinned, almond-colored beauty, was funny and sweet and the two little girls were inseparable.

Elaine took delight in teaching Trixie to read and write, even though she knew it to be strictly forbidden. She helped her playmate learn to speak properly, coaching her to lose the 'slave talk' that the other black children spoke.

"My mama said I could never tell anyone that I can read and write," Trixie told Elaine.

It was warm summer day and they were sitting in their secret hiding place in the meadow behind the stables. "She looked really scairt when I showed her I could write my name. She threw the paper in the cookstove!"

"'Scared,'" corrected Elaine. "Well, I just don't understand what the fuss is all about. A body ought to be able to learn to read and write if they want to!" Elaine's temper flared as she thought of the meanness of some grown-ups. She didn't believe her mama and papa would care one whit if they knew that Trixie could read. Still, somehow, she didn't feel comfortable telling them.

As they grew into their teen years, her relationship with Trixie and her other black friends began to change. Nanny said it wasn't "pro'prit' for a 'growed up' white gal to 'so-shate' wid de black servants." Since that was "jest de way things is," Elaine reluctantly accepted it, moving into the whirlwind of young adulthood in the St. Louis high society. Though she still tried to be friendly with Trixie, slowly an unavoidable barrier began to come up between them, and her childhood friend seemed to deliberately keep her distance.

As time went by, Elaine noticed Trixie became more and more reserved. It seemed she was always on the verge of saying something but never gave herself the liberty to do so.

One afternoon, Elaine happened upon Trixie in the breezeway that connected the main house to the kitchen. Imogene had put her daughter to peeling potatoes for dinner and she had sought out the coolness of the breezeway for the task.

"Hello, Trixie." Elaine spoke cordially and smiled at her black friend. Trixie didn't look up from the pan as she grunted an unintelligible reply.

"Trixie, I'm going to ask you a question, and I want you to answer me honestly. Why aren't you friendly to me anymore? You're always so stand-offish and cold," said Elaine, baring her feelings to her childhood friend.

Still keeping her head bent to her task, Trixie mumbled, "Ah don't know whut you mean, Missy."

Elaine felt shocked at Trixie's use of "slave talk." She hadn't heard her speak that way since they were both very small children. "Why, Trixie, why are you talking that way?"

"Ah don't know whut you talkin' 'bout, Missy. Ah's jist talkin' lak all us dahkies talk!"

Exasperated, Elaine said, "Trixie, please stop peeling those silly potatoes this instant and look at me!"

Slowly, Trixie did as she was told, her face sullen.

"Now, tell me why you aren't friendly anymore and why you're speaking in that ridiculous fashion when we both know you can speak as well as any white person?" Elaine softened her tone. "We were so close once. We shared secrets and I thought we had a special relationship. What happened to make you so angry with me?" Elaine sat down on the step just below Trixie and looked her in the eye.

"Yas'm, we wuz close onct, but dat were a long time ago. Thangs change."

"I know how you feel, Trixie, but—" Elaine began, only to be interrupted by Trixie, who in a very cold, deliberate tone, left no doubt in anyone's mind that their relationship had definitely changed. "Dere ain't no way you could *ever* know how a black gal feel, Missy. No way in dis worl.' Ah's very sorry, Missy, if'n Ah has offended you. Ah knows my place around hyar and Ah would not step out of it. You ain't done nothing' dat Ah knows of, Miss 'laine." She dropped her head and began her task again.

"Very well, Trixie. If that's the way you want it." Still confused and sad, Elaine walked away.

CHAPTER 2

A HANDSOME GELDING STOOD WITH his head drooped sleepily at the hitching rail in front of the Denton home. A gaudy, ornate harness hitched him to a luxurious buggy, complete with soft leather seats and a canopy with fringe that shimmied in the breeze.

Two young people sat side by side on a bench underneath a massive oak tree which shaded most of the Denton front yard. The girl quickly turned her back on her lovesick companion and gazed intently out across the wide expanse of the mighty Mississippi. The fringe on her dainty parasol jiggled and shivered with her movement. She bit her lower lip and tried not to laugh. Michael Tolbert was such a ninny!

"Oh, Elaine, I'm so sorry! I didn't mean to embarrass you, honest, I didn't! But I do love you so!" Timidly, Michael reached out to take her hand, but Elaine snatched it away.

Coolly, she looked at him. In her most theatrical, condescending tone, she said, "Michael, you and I have nothing in common. I don't love you and I never shall. What you want can never be!" She put a placating hand on his arm. "Please, you must leave now and it would be best if you do not call again. I'm sorry." With that, she regally took her exit and, once inside, hurried up to her room.

The poor, rejected suitor bowed to her retreat. Red-faced and miserable, he took his leave. He knew why she wouldn't have him as her beau. She didn't think he was good enough for her. He'd change her mind someday. She'd come to love him as he loved her. She had to. Michael felt a sense of frustration, akin to desperation, set in.

Upstairs, Elaine looked out her bedroom window to the dejected young man climbing into his carriage. "Look, Nanny!" she said to the hefty black woman who had taken care of her since the day she was born. "Doesn't he look rather like a grasshopper crawling into that buggy?" Elaine giggled at her own wit.

"He mostly elbows and knees, all right, Missy," she replied. "Anyways, he jist pore white trash. Don' know why he think he kin court de purtiest gal in dis hyar county." Nanny sniffed knowingly as she continued in her infinite wisdom of such matters. "'Most ever'one knows you is gwine to marry up wid some fine gennelman one o' dese days, an' not wid de likes o' him, an' dat's a fac'!"

Nanny had become used to the steady stream of bachelors storming the big house overlooking the river since her charge turned sixteen two years ago last spring. Each one hoped to unlock the heart of the beautiful Elaine Denton. She was quick to express her opinion of each suitor, and to date, not one had been good enough for her "Missy."

Elaine's father owned several warehouses on the riverfront, as well as being vice president of a local branch of one of the few banks allowed to operate in Missouri at that time. Ralph and Blanche had a plan drawn out for their daughter's future, and this had become a source of great irritation to their strong-willed daughter. It was only a matter of time until one in the parade of young men would turn her head and she would marry. They intended that she should marry well. Only a son from an old established family would do. Education, prestige, family, position, and wealth—all of these were terribly important qualities for their future son-in-law to possess. They had made no secret that they hoped she would marry Jeremy Craig. His father owned one of the largest fleets of riverboats in St. Louis. The Denton Enterprises and the Craig Riverboat Company would make a very good match indeed! A young man such as the

Tolbert boy did not fit the pattern at all, and her parents would be pleased to hear that she had become bored and sent him away.

Michael's parents, Mitch and Nellie Tolbert, were the antithesis of Ralph and Blanche Denton. Both were uneducated, crude, and lusting for the type of life that they had only been able to dream about until recently. Mitch, a vulgar, cursing, tobacco spitting, seldom-bathing son of a Kentucky farmer, had been a fur trapper in years past. Because of some lucky breaks and his many illegal dealings, he began to find himself in a position of affluence. His wife, Nellie, was a mousy little woman with a high-pitched nasal twang. Her voice grated unpleasantly on the listener's ears. Both were a source of great embarrassment for the pompous, spoiled son they had produced.

Gradually, Tolbert's business grew to the point that he decided he had enough wealth to be a match for those "long-nosed blue bloods in St. Looey!" He bought himself some flashy duds and dressed Nellie in equally gaudy attire. He bought one of the largest homes in St. Louis and had it furnished extravagantly, all in poor taste, according to the gossip from those who had observed it. Everything he bought dripped with baubles, bangles, and garish poor taste. He thought that if he paid a lot of money for it, if it shined brighter and loomed larger than anything everyone else had, it must surely earn him respect in the St. Louis social elite circle. He felt the elite would respect his money, if nothing else. He found that to be partially true, but not to the extent he wished.

When Michael came along, they took pains to see to it that his education was the best that money could buy. They spoiled him beyond belief so that he became a selfish brat. As he grew into manhood, Michael maintained his self-indulgent lifestyle, never knowing what it was like to want something and not be able to have it. That is, until he saw Elaine Denton at a picnic one Sunday afternoon. Her red hair glowed copper in the sunlight and he felt himself drowning in the deep hazel well of her eyes. He thought he had never seen a girl so beautiful! On the spot, he made up his mind that someday she would become Mrs. Michael Tolbert. Michael had made the mistake of mentioning Elaine's beauty to his mother. The memory of her encounter with Blanche Denton would always bring a flush of anger and mortification to him.

Nellie walked over to Blanche, who stood, dainty parasol in one hand and a glass of lemonade in the other, watching a group of children competing in a sack race. "How do, Missus," Nellie's nasally voice twanged to Blanche. Politely, Blanche had acknowledged the greeting. "My boy Michael, he's plum tuk a shine to yore redhead. I do b'lieve that boy's done set his cap fer her!" Her loud raucous laughter made heads turn their way.

Coolly, Blanche replied, "My dear Mrs. Tolbert, I assure you that relationship will never happen. My daughter is a well-bred, lovely, refined young lady. I'm afraid your Michael should look elsewhere. Now, if you'll excuse me."

Nellie's voice followed Blanche as she made her dignified departure. "Hoity-toity, that's what you ere! Highfalutin! You jist think yore gal is too good for my Michael! Well, she ain't! He can have his pick of any gal in this city! At least my boy ain't got no darky fer a sister!" Michael was mortified as he overheard his mother's outburst. He quickly grabbed her arm and unceremoniously loaded her into the buggy. As they drove away, he could see people whispering behind their hands and pointing their direction. He needed a drink.

Coolly, and with dignity, Blanche called to Elaine. "Gather up your things, dahlin.' We need to be goin' home now."

Elaine climbed into the carriage beside her mother and watched as Ramsey loaded the picnic basket and blankets. As they drove off, Elaine turned to Blanche and asked quietly, "Mama, what did that horrible woman mean about Michael not having a—?"

"Oh, my goodness, girl!" Blanche sputtered. "She was just talkin' to hear the sound of her own voice!" Blanche fanned herself furiously.

"No, Mama, I saw it in your face when she said it. What is it all about?" Elaine pleaded.

"I don't want to talk about this again, not now or ever! One doesn't speak of certain things, my dear," she said more gently. "Genteel ladies have certain crosses to bear and we bear them in silence. This is one of those things and I will not discuss it. Do not ask me about it again, do you hear me, child?"

Bewildered, Elaine whispered, "Yes, Mama." Resolutely, she determined to put the unpleasantness behind her and forget about it. She couldn't remember ever having seen her mother so upset.

CHAPTER 3

THE DENTONS ALWAYS DRESSED FORMALLY for the evening meal. "My dear," Blanche said to her husband in her soft, Southern drawl, "I've told Imogene to plan for dinner for twelve this evenin'. Do be a love and wear that blue brocade cravat I gave you for Christmas. It makes you look so distinguished." She gave him a wifely peck on the cheek. "I'm goin' to go talk to Elaine. The Craigs are among the guests I have invited." They looked knowingly at one another. Further comments weren't needed. They both knew how their high-strung daughter felt about their matchmaking. They felt sure, however, just given time and getting better acquainted, that the two young people would eventually succumb to the inevitable.

The woman who walked down the hall toward her daughter's room radiated natural beauty and grace, although Father Time had begun to take his toll. She could no longer boast of the tiniest waist in St. Louis, but the silver in her hair gave her face a luminescence. Blanche Renault Denton was very French, her New Orleans heritage obvious in her refined drawl. Politely, she knocked on Elaine's door. "Dahlin', may I come in?"

"Of, course, Mama! Please do!" Blanche heard barely concealed excitement in her daughter's voice.

As Blanche entered, her gaze swept the very feminine room and she saw a wide-eyed little black boy, hat in hand, shuffling from one foot to the other, standing just inside the door. "Well, what have we here?" she asked.

Elaine said, "Guess what, Mama? Amanda's boy just brought a note inviting me to a sleepover, and she wants me to attend her at the Coming-Out Ball next month! Isn't that just splendid?" Amanda had been Elaine's attendant when she "came ou," standing with her in the spectacular receiving line and giving her moral support.

The annual Debutantes' Ball was held each March for the express purpose of launching the sixteen-year-old daughters of the wealthy families in the area into a whirlwind of social activity. As a result, each young lady hoped to meet a suitable beau and marry well. These were the "old money" families. The "vulgar rich," as they were referred to, were not welcome at this momentous occasion. The last thing they wanted was for one of their daughters to marry one of "them."

Even so, after a young lady "came out," all the eligible young men came calling at their front doors, including some from the less desirable families.

"That's wonderful, dahlin'. I know you will make a beautiful attendant, but I'm afraid you can't make the sleepover tonight. We're having dinner guests, and I know they would be dreadfully disappointed if they didn't get to see our best girl!" said Blanche sweetly.

Suspicion crowded her daughter's eyes. "Who's coming, Mama?" she asked in a deceptively calm voice.

"Well, there's Dr. Martin and his wife, Mr. and Mrs. Levitt, the Thorntons and—"

"And the Craigs?" broke in Elaine.

"Why, yes, dear, as a matter of fact, I did ask the Craigs," replied Blanche, trying to look nonchalant, but steeling herself for the outburst she saw coming.

"Mama! You and Papa are at it again, aren't you? How could you just keep throwing Jeremy Craig at me like that? He's a very polite fellow and is nice enough, I suppose, but I could never love him! It's so humiliating the way you keep asking him over. I feel like a cow on an auction block!" Elaine's voice rose higher and higher as she spoke until she burst into tears.

Genuine shock registered on her mother's face. Manipulating though she was, she really loved her daughter very much. "My dahlin' girl, your father and I would never bargain with your future. We only want what's best for you. That's all we want, don't you see?"

Petulantly, Elaine picked up a pencil and paper and hurriedly jotted down a note. She handed it to the uncomfortable boy who touched the brim of his hat politely and quickly made his exit. "Nanny, pack my things." The rebellious girl turned to her mother. "Mama, I'm going to Amanda's. I'll be home day after tomorrow." She sniffed and Nanny handed her a dainty handkerchief.

Blanche took a good look at her obstinate daughter. She recognized the stubborn set to her jaw and knew that no amount of coaxing would change her mind. She also knew if she forbade her to go that there was no telling what the headstrong girl would do or say to the Craig's at dinner that night. With a sigh, Blanche conceded defeat. "Very well, dahlin', if you feel that strongly about it, run on to Amanda's if you like." As she left the room she called back over her shoulder, "We'll have the Craigs over again in a couple of weeks." A plaintive "Ma-ma!" followed her down the hall.

CHAPTER 4

WHEN RAMSEY STOPPED THE CARRIAGE in front of the Hathcock mansion, the front door flew open and Amanda came tearing down the steps to greet her friend. Elaine caught a glimpse of a black woman scowling at the excited girl from the doorway. She figured Amanda would be in for a tongue-lashing from her nanny about her lack of decorum. "Ladies don' run! Dey hurries wid dignity!" her own nanny had told her over and over.

Elaine laughed as she and Amanda embraced, both chattering at once. "Did you bring your gown?" "What color is yours?" "I can't wait for the Ball, can you?"

Later that evening the girls sat in the middle of Amanda's huge four-poster bed, each of them in flannel nightgowns and ruffled sleeping caps. They were speaking almost in whispers so no one would know they were staying up so late.

"Oh, Mandy, I'm so glad you invited me over! Mama and Papa invited Jeremy Craig over tonight for supper!" Elaine's red hair fairly crackled as she got angry all over again at the thought. "Why would they just keep pushing him at me like that?"

"Well, he *is* quite handsome, don't you think?" Amanda dropped her eyes as she spoke, and it suddenly occurred to Elaine that her friend might have more than a passing interest in Jeremy.

"Why, you sly thing! You're sweet on him, aren't you?" Elaine saw the red slowly spread from Amanda's face, down her neck, disappearing into the ruffle of her yellow nightgown.

"No, of course not! Why would you ever think so?" sputtered Amanda, still avoiding her friend's eyes.

"Amanda Hathcock! Look at me!" commanded Elaine. Slowly Amanda met her eyes. "You *are* sweet on him, aren't you?"

Dropping all pretense, Amanda sighed. "I suppose I am, but please, *please* don't you tell, Elaine Denton! I'll just be mortified if you do! He doesn't even know I'm alive, and I can't figure out how to get his attention!"

For a long time the girls schemed and planned on how to get the elusive Mr. Jeremy Craig to focus his attention on Amanda.

There came a brief lull in the conversation and Elaine could feel the tiredness start to creep in. Suddenly, Amanda sat straight up. "Oh my goodness!" she exclaimed, almost scaring Elaine out of ten year's growth!

"What? What's wrong?" she asked with alarm.

"I'm so nervous about getting up in front of all those people at the ball," wailed Amanda. "What if I make a mistake? What if I trip when I come down the steps? And *he'll* be there!" The poor girl worked herself into a state. "Oh my goodness! I just don't think I can do it!"

Elaine patted her friend's hands. "You were right there with me when I "came out." You weren't nervous then! What happened?"

"Well, *you* were the center of attention then, and I was only the attendant. I figured everyone was looking at you and not at me!" She smiled in her shy way.

"You'll do everything just right, Mandy. Don't you fret," Elaine reassured her. "Besides, if you trip you'll fall into the girl ahead of you, and it will be just like Dominoes!" The girls giggled out loud at the thought. Suddenly, a voice came down the hall, "Turn out the lamp, girls, and settle down now! It's time to go to sleep!" They turned out the lamp immediately, but it was a several minutes and a couple more stern reminders from down the hall before the giggles subsided and the room became silent as the girls drifted into a dreamless sleep!

The next morning broke crystal clear, the sun shining magnificently. "Would you like to take a ride this morning, Elaine?" Amanda asked her friend. "I'll ask Papa for the carriage, and we can take a picnic lunch down by the river!"

"Oh, that would be lovely! Let's do!" Amanda got permission from her father to borrow the carriage for the day and put the servants to packing a nice picnic lunch.

They had the driver take them downtown where they did some shopping. Gaily they went down to the park on a bluff overlooking the Mississippi. They found a nice spot in the warm sunshine to spread out their picnic, for although the sun was bright, the wind was a bit brisk.

As they were enjoying their lunch, Michael Tolbert rode up to them and tipped his hat. "Good afternoon, ladies," he said with a smile. "Looks like you're having a grand time!"

Coolly, they nodded and agreed that they were, indeed, having a good time. There was an awkward pause.

Michael cleared his throat and said, "Elaine, uh—Miss Denton—I need to speak to you privately for just a moment, if I may."

"Michael, I told you the other day that—" Elaine began.

"Please, just for a moment. I must ask you something." Michael practically begged.

"Oh, for goodness sake!" said Elaine ungraciously. "All right! Amanda, we'll just walk a little way. I won't go far."

Amanda nodded uncertainly.

Michael got down from the big gelding and reached down to help Elaine to get up. She snatched her hand from his and they walked slowly across the lawn until they were out of earshot of Amanda.

"Miss Denton, Elaine, I—well, I just wanted to tell you how terribly sorry I am for those awful things my mother said to yours the other day." He beseeched her. "Can you ever forgive me?"

"There's nothing to forgive *you* for," she retorted. "You aren't the one who made a scene."

"I know, but she is my mother and I feel responsible. I just don't want you to be angry with me over it," he said pleadingly.

Elaine looked at the miserable young man in front of her. She reached out and placed her hand on his arm. "I tell you what. I'll forgive you if you'll tell me what your mother meant when she said, 'At least my boy doesn't have a darky for a sister.'"

Michael squirmed visibly. "Elaine, please don't ask me about that. I just don't want you to be angry with me, that's all."

She squeezed his arm as hard as she could. "Michael, I will only be able to forgive you if you tell me what I want to know. Now, what did she mean?" Elaine's heart was pounding for some reason as she waited to hear his answer.

Michael hung his head. "Just remember, I don't want to tell you. You are forcing me to tell you something that I know will only hurt you."

"Michael, what is it?" Elaine's voice had dropped to a whisper.

"It is common knowledge around town that the light-skinned slave your father owns—"

"You mean Trixie? About my age?" interrupted Elaine. Michael nodded. "She is our cook's daughter."

"Do you know who her father is?"

"Well, no, I can't say as I ever heard anyone say who her father is," replied Elaine, her voice soft and her heart pounding harder now.

"You know, don't you?" Michael asked. "Can't you figure it out without me having to say it?"

"Say it, Michael," she demanded through clenched teeth.

Miserably, Michael told her what she suspected all along but couldn't bring herself to believe. "Trixie's your half-sister. Your father is her father."

Elaine slapped him so hard his ears rang. "Liar! Liar!" she screamed and ran back to Amanda. "I want to go home. Please take me home right now!" she cried.

Amanda put her arms around her friend and watched as Michael slowly mounted his horse and rode away.

"What did he say to you?" asked Amanda, "We'll go home and tell my Papa!" Amanda looked with dismay at her hysterical friend.

"Please, Amanda, I—I can't talk about it right now. There's nothing your father can do. Just take me home now, please!" begged Elaine.

Without another word, her friend directed their driver to pick up the picnic items and the blanket and they got into the buggy and drove the short distance to the Denton home.

When Elaine burst into the living room, she heard the strains of a beautiful tune being played on the piano. She rushed over and grabbed her mother by the shoulders, sobbing great gasping sobs. "Mama! Please tell me the truth!"

Alarmed, Blanche stood and tried to get calm her daughter. "Why, whatever is the matter, dahlin'? What is it, child?"

As though someone had thrown cold water on her, Elaine became very calm. Looking her mother in the eye, she said, "Tell me who Trixie's father is."

"Why, I told you the other day at the park that there are certain things ladies do not discuss—"

"Mama. Is Papa her father?" Elaine actually shook Blanche. "Is he?"

Dropping all pretense, Blanche simply said, "Yes." Prying her daughter's fingers from her arms, Blanche pleaded, "Please, dahlin', you're hurting me."

Elaine released her mother and ran to her room, ignoring her mother's frantic pleading to allow her to explain.

Elaine refused to come down for dinner, and about nine o'clock that evening, Ralph lightly tapped on his daughter's door. "May I come in, honey?"

"No! Go away, Papa! I just can't talk to you right now."

"We need to talk about this, Elaine," he said in a little sterner voice. Only silence answered from inside the room. He jiggled the doorknob, but it was locked. With a defeated sag to his shoulders, Ralph Denton walked away.

CHAPTER 5

S PARKLING CHANDELIERS LIT UP THE huge ballroom in the prestigious Planter's Hotel. Long streamers and gay banners fluttered all around the room. At one end were tables laden with food. Hors d'oeuvres, cake, punch, fruit, and fancy ices were arranged temptingly, with as much ingenuity as the chefs could muster.

At the other end of the ballroom, on a raised dais, an orchestra tuned up for the gala event. Behind the orchestra, a curtained stage hid the twittering, giggling debutantes and their attendants. Anticipation rose to a peak as the girls shuffled about nervously, powdering their noses, arranging their corsages, and fanning themselves. Elaine put the finishing touches to Amanda's hair and they opened the stage door and joined the others. An expectant hush fell over the crowd as the trumpets began the fanfare and His Honor, John Dumond, the mayor of St. Louis, made his way to the podium. After an excruciatingly long welcome speech, he began calling out the names of the debutantes and their attendants, in his own pompous way.

Amanda grabbed Elaine's hand. "I just don't think I can go through with this!"

Elaine realized her friend was close to fainting with nervousness. "Relax, Mandy! There's really nothing to it! When I 'came out.' I thought it ever so much fun!" She leaned over and gave the terrified girl a hug and a little shake. "Come on! Your dress is just scrumptious and you do look elegant!"

Just then, they heard the mayor say, "It is my pleasure to present to you Miss Amanda Hathcock, daughter of Mr. and Mrs. John Hathcock, and her attendant, Miss Elaine Denton, daughter of Mr. and Mrs. Ralph Denton." As though in a dream, Amanda walked gracefully forward, curtseying to His Honor, then to the applauding crowd. Elaine followed a few discreet steps behind her, also acknowledging the mayor and then the crowd with an elegant curtsey. They descended the steps to the ballroom floor where escorts were waiting to lead them to the twittering line of girls who made a frilly, fluffy, lacy receiving line.

Suddenly Amanda grabbed Elaine's arm. In a hysterical whisper she said, "Oh, my goodness! I am such a goose! I have gone and left my dance card in the dressing room!"

Soothingly Elaine told her nervous friend that she would go get it for her.

Trying to be as inconspicuous as possible, Elaine hurried out of the ballroom and down the now empty corridor to the dressing room she and Amanda had shared earlier with a flurry of other debutantes. There lay the forgotten dance card on the dressing table. She snatched it up and started back quickly toward the ballroom.

From out of the shadows, Michael Tolbert materialized in front of her. He lurched toward her, grabbing both her wrists in a viselike grip. He pulled her up to him, and she could smell the liquor on his breath. "I saw you leave the ballroom and I followed you back here." He smiled a crooked drunken smile. "How about a li'l kiss?" Elaine struggled with all her might but couldn't disentangle herself from his clutches. "Michael, what are you doing here? How did you get in?" Getting more frightened, she begged, "Please, Michael! Let me go!" she demanded. "You're hurting me!" she said through clinched teeth.

"I believe the lady would like fer ya ta turn 'er loose." The voice was deep and stern. Elaine looked around and stared into the bluest pair of eyes she had ever seen! Blond, curly hair peeked out from under his hat as though it had been captured under protest. He was tall, so tall that Elaine had to lean her head back to see his face.

Handsome in a rugged way, his square jaw said 'no nonsense.' He stared down at Michael, his blue eyes steely.

"Mind your own business, Hick!" spat Michael.

Blue Eyes immediately wrenched Elaine from his grip and punched him in the nose. Michael fell with a crash, his nose bleeding profusely. He drew out a white handkerchief and held it to the offended appendage. "Now, if ya know what's good fer ya, you'll git on outta here, *now*!" Michael stood and slunk out the door like a whipped animal.

"Looks like me and ma friends got here jist in the nick'a time," he said with a smile. "Are ya all right, miss?"

"Y-yes, yes, I'm fine, thank you so much!" replied Elaine rubbing, her wrists where Michael had been holding her. At the mention of his friends, Elaine realized that Blue Eyes did indeed have two fellows with him.

One of them said, in a wheedling tone, "Now, ya ain't gonna tell on us are ya, Miss? Like Lonnie says, we jist come over ta see what all the fuss is about. And 'specially since he went and whupped up on him that was a'botherin' ya and all."

Lonnie. That was his name. Elaine knew she should ask them to leave, for uninvited guests were not welcome at these cliquish functions. Three big strapping country boys like these fellows would definitely stand out in their Sunday-go-to-meeting clothes.

With great dignity and indifference Elaine replied, "I won't tell, but I won't have to. Somebody else will spot you, and you'll be thrown out in front of everyone."

She looked up into Lonnie Blue Eyes' face and suddenly found herself stammering. "Uh-well-I-I-uh must go on out to the ballroom. My friend is waiting for me." She pushed on the stage door, but it wouldn't open. She tried again, but it seemed to be jammed. With her embarrassment mounting, she pushed once again, but it still wouldn't budge.

A big steady hand touched her elbow and Lonnie Blue Eyes said kindly, "Let me do that fer ya, Miss." To her utter chagrin he reached down and *pulled* the door open! Her face beet-red, she mumbled her thanks and practically ran into the ballroom, promptly crashing into Jeremy Craig.

"Excuse me!" they both said at the same time. Just then, the orchestra began the first dance of the evening, a beautiful Strauss waltz. "Where were you?" Jeremy asked rather testily. I've been looking for you. I'm supposed to have the first dance, you know," he finished smugly. Elaine did know, and she was still furious that her mother had arranged for Jeremy to be her escort for this evening. Jeremy, on the other hand, felt Elaine should be grateful that she had the honor of being escorted by him.

Everyone waited as the honored debutantes and their partners swept across the floor, twirling 'round and 'round in time to the beautiful waltz. After all the debutants were dancing, their attendants and their partners took to the floor. Then one by one the other couples joined in. With a slight bow to Elaine, Jeremy said, "Shall we?"

"Certainly, thank you!" replied Elaine demurely, trying to regain her composure.

She thought to herself that Jeremy Craig could do *something* to please her, for he could dance beautifully.

A pang of conscience struck her as she saw the sadness in Amanda's eyes as they danced by her friend and her partner, George Friedman. Elaine thought they both looked as though they would rather be anywhere else. "I'm not feeling very well, Jeremy. Why don't you go cut in on Amanda while I catch my breath?"

"Are you all right?" he asked with concern.

"Yes, yes, I'll be fine. I just feel like I need some air. Please do ask Amanda to dance. This song is one of her favorites, I know, and you dance so nicely." Conspiratorially she whispered, "I think she needs rescue."

Looking a little confused but pleased with the compliment, he did as she asked. He lightly tapped poor George on the shoulder and cut in to finish the beautiful waltz with a glowing Amanda. George, somewhat overweight, was red-faced and sweating unpleasantly with the exertion of the dance. He gratefully removed Amanda's hand from his own sweaty one and placed it into Jeremy's outstretched palm. Immediately, he headed for the refreshment table. Elaine couldn't help but stifle a giggle.

Jeremy really was a marvelous dancer, and he and Amanda made a striking couple as they dipped and twirled and swayed to the music. Elaine felt glad for her friend. Belatedly, she realized she'd failed to give her the elusive dance card.

She caught a glimpse of three uncomfortable, rather furtive-looking fellows, one of them with piercing blue eyes, making their way toward the refreshment tables as well. Moments later, Elaine was aghast when Lonnie Blue Eyes came over, as cool as a cucumber, and asked her to dance! Stunned, she took his hand and moved with him onto the dance floor, but before they could take the first step, the orchestra played the closing strains of the beautiful piece and thunderous applause shook the ballroom.

Spotting Amanda across the room, Elaine excused herself and started toward her. She realized the blue-eyed stranger was right behind her! As they approached Amanda, Elaine handed the dance card to her. Jeremy glared at Lonnie Blue Eyes. Ignoring Jeremy, Lonnie looked at her and grinned. "Whew!" What luck! I was wonderin' what I was gonna do, 'cause I'm sure not much of a dancer!"

Elaine tried to look contemptuous. "Well, then, sir, why did you ask me at *all* if you can't dance?"

Lonnie took her arm and guided her to a side door that went out onto a big, full-length terrace that covered the front of the hotel. There were colored lanterns and tables decorated with flowers. Other couples, too, were coming out to get a breath of fresh air after the dance.

"Because, Miss—" "Say, what *is* yore name anyway?" he asked, suddenly realizing he didn't know.

"Why, it's Elaine. Elaine Denton," she said.

"Well, Miss Elaine Denton, I asked ya because I think yore the *purtiest* girl I've ever laid eyes on!"

Elaine again felt the rush of blood to her cheeks. She didn't know this fellow at all, and he seemed to have the knack of turning her into a stammering idiot. "W-well, I don't know *your* name or who your f-family is or anything about you either!" she blurted.

"My name is Lonnie Ross, Miss Elaine Denton, and I'm very pleased to make yore acquaintance. As ta who I am, why—I'm jist me! I ain't nobody in particular, I don't guess, but jist as good as any man here." He said the last statement with some defiance, as though daring her to deny it.

"I'm sure you are, I mean, well, I just meant who is your family and where *do* you live? Is your father's business here in St. Louis or—?"

Lonnie cut her short. "My 'father' lit out on Ma and me before I was even born! We've been scratchin' a livin' out on a little no-account piece a' land over on the Illinois side—that is, until last May." Quickly, Lonnie turned his head, but not before Elaine caught the glint of tears in those blue eyes of his.

"What happened last May, Lonnie?" she asked softly.

Lonnie took a deep breath. "Ma died and the bank took our place. Now, I don't have nothin' or nobody." He realized with sudden embarrassment how personal he had become with this spoiled little rich girl. He could imagine himself the subject of a good laugh with her other spoiled little rich girl friends later. "I ain't complainin', mind ya," his former bravado returning, "'cause I'm fixin' ta do something I've wanted ta do my whole life. I'm goin' west."

He said the words with reverence, much as one would say, 'I'm going to heaven.' "I'm goin' ta Oregon and I'm gonna find me a green valley under one'a those big old snow-covered mountains and make myself a home right there!"

Elaine's pulse raced! His excitement was contagious! To go out west, to a brand-new land and make a home, what an adventure that would be for this unusual young man! "When will you be leaving?" she asked softly.

"In about six weeks, after the spring thaw," he replied. Suddenly those blue eyes locked into her hazel ones. "Can I come ta see ya before I go?"

The unexpected question left Elaine speechless and before she could find her tongue, they both became aware of a situation taking place inside. The orchestra was between numbers and angry voices floated plainly from inside the crowded ballroom. "—have to leave!" "—uninvited yokels!" Then the sound of a blow being delivered to someone's jaw and the crash of chairs and breaking glass came loud and clear. Ladies began screaming, and everyone ran back inside to see what was happening.

With clenched fists, Lonnie started for the door, intent on helping his friends, but Elaine grabbed his arm. "Lonnie, don't go in there, please! By the sound of things, it's all over anyway." For reasons she couldn't explain, she didn't want her big blue-eyed companion to go charging into the ballroom and be humiliated by the aristocratic snobs who were inside. She had seen them at work before and knew how vicious they could be.

Stubbornly, Lonnie set his feet. "My friends are in trouble. I gotta go help 'em." He said the words slowly, as though to a child.

Before she could reply, Lonnie's two friends came flying out onto the veranda, sprawling at the feet of their big friend. Two good-sized fellows in expensive suits tossed the intruder's hats out to them. "You forgot something, *gentlemen!*" one of them jeered, and Elaine recognized Jeremy Craig's voice.

Lonnie sauntered up to the door where the young men stood, tilting his head downward slightly to stare Jeremy in the eye.

"Well, well." Jeremy sneered. "If it isn't Sir Galahad!" Turning to Elaine, he asked, "What are you doing out here with him?" He grabbed her arm as though to lead her away.

"Miss Denton is a big girl, my friend!" Lonnie shot back. "I think it best if ya just let her decide if she wants ta be out here or not."

Elaine shook her arm free from Jeremy's grip and pushed between the two, for by this time, they were practically toe to toe.

"Now, just a minute, you two. I can speak for myself!" Whirling to face Jeremy, she snapped, "Jeremy Craig, I don't need you to tell me who my friends are. It just so happens that these young men *are* friends of mine and here at my invitation! Now, apologize or I shall be forced to leave."

Jeremy's mouth dropped open. Incredulously he croaked, "Friends of *yours*? Apologize? Don't be ridiculous, Elaine! They don't have invitations! You know the rules! They can't come in without one!" Seeing her obstinate look, Jeremy took her tightly clinched fists in his hands. "Elaine, I'm not about to apologize. How can you take their side? You don't even know them! You can't expect me to believe that you actually invited them?"

Elaine drew herself up to her full five feet, and her red hair fairly crackled with anger. Shaking her arm free from Jeremy's grip, she turned to Lonnie, saying sweetly, "I'm ready to go home now. Will you gentlemen be so kind as to escort me?"

"But, Elaine," Jeremy protested, "*I'm* supposed to be your escort!" He took her elbow with a firm grip. She looked at his hand on her elbow then slowly raised her eyes to meet his with an icy stare. A deep red flush spread upward into Jeremy's hairline, and reluctantly he removed his hand and walked away with as much bravado as he could muster.

Elaine took Lonnie's arm and the arm of one of his friends whose names she still did not know. With the third young man bringing up the rear, the little entourage made its way off the veranda and over to the large covered receiving area in front of the hotel. Elaine pointed out to the street where Ramsey waited with the carriage and asked if one of them would care to get his attention. A shrill whistle broke through the quiet evening and startled, Ramsey turned to find its source. Elaine waved for him to come up and get them.

Ramsey pulled up to where Elaine was standing and watched with dismay as his mistress entered the carriage with three strange young men. "Marse Ralph shorely ain't goin' to like dis," he mumbled to himself. Meanwhile, Amanda and the whole crowd watched, open-mouthed, as the little group entered the carriage and drove away.

Lonnie and Elaine sat on one side of the carriage and the other two young men were seated opposite them. "Miss Elaine, these are my friends, Matthew Jones and Billie Thompson." The young men smiled and touched their hat brims respectfully. "How do, ma'am," they both said at once.

Nervously, Elaine smiled and nodded back. What in the world had she done? Would she ever learn to control her temper? Now here she sat in a carriage full of strangers all by herself. She knew she should be afraid, but for some reason, sitting here beside Lonnie, she felt safe.

They pulled up to the address they'd given Ramsey and Matt and Billie got out, bidding Elaine good night. "I'll see the lady home and be back in a little while," Lonnie told them. Tipping their hats to Elaine, they nodded to Lonnie and went inside.

Ramsey pulled up in front of the Denton home. Lonnie just sat there, not saying anything for a bit, then gently he reached for her hand. "Ya know I told ya I'm leavin' in just a few short weeks, but I want ta get ta know ya better. I know it's crazy, I feel like I do know ya—aw, heck, I guess what I'm tryin' ta say is, can I call on ya?"

She did know what he meant, for she felt the same way—a familiarity and comfortableness with this young stranger that she didn't understand. Elaine knew she should decline politely but somehow she couldn't. She had to see him again, to know more about this gentle blue-eyed young man who had suddenly thrust himself into her life. She found herself saying, "Yes, I'd like to see you again."

His smile was quick and wonderful. "I'll come by tomorrow afternoon and pick ya up fer a ride. Is two o'clock okay?" Her next words caused the smile to vanish as she said, "Why don't I just meet you down by the river? I go riding every day and—"

"What ya mean is, ya don't want me comin' ta yore house. Ain't that right?"

Too quickly, she answered, "Oh, that's not it at all. I just thought meeting you down by the river would be more convenient for you." She couldn't meet his eyes.

"All right. I'll meet ya in Barrett's Cove tomorrow about one o'clock." Disappointment filled his eyes as he squeezed her hand and exited the carriage.

"Lonnie, wait!" she exclaimed. "Let Ramsey drive you back to your hotel!"

"Aw, that's all right," he answered. "I'll just walk back. It's not far and I got some thinkin' ta do." He tipped his hat, and with a few long strides of those long legs of his, he was out of sight.

CHAPTER 6

After lunch the next day, Elaine dressed in her riding clothes and went out to the stables where Ramsey had her mare saddled and waiting. "Thank you, Ramsey. I'll be back soon." she said as she rode off.

"Yas'm, Missy, you has you a good ride!" Ramsey called after her.

The closer to Barrett's Cove she rode, the more nervous she became. She didn't know this man she was about to meet in a deserted place. What if he was a murderer who took advantage of unsuspecting, foolish young ladies who met him at the river? She had just about decided to turn around and go back home when Lonnie came riding up beside her on a big bay horse. "Afternoon!" he said with a smile that totally wiped away all her fears. "That old river looks mighty fine out there, don't it?'

"Yes, I love the river," she answered. They rode into the cove and dismounted, sitting side by side on a big boulder. In awkward silence, they sat gazing at the river.

Lonnie finally broke the silence. "Why did you agree ta meet me?" he asked her.

"Honestly, I don't know," she answered shyly.

"Must-a been my manly charm!" he joked, and they laughed. That seemed to melt the ice and they both began to talk, their words tumbling over each other as they raced to learn all they could about each other. After all, they didn't have much time before he would be leaving for Oregon.

The sun was low in the sky when Elaine returned home from her ride. She walked into the living room and realized immediately that something was wrong. It didn't take her father long to fill in the details. When her parents heard of the incident at the ball (Jeremy Craig's mother had made a beeline to tell them) they were shocked beyond words. Blanche had taken to her bed with fainting spells every time the subject came up, and Ralph went into long tirades about challenging them to a duel, or perhaps calling the constable and having them arrested if they dared to show their faces around his daughter again!

"Elaine, what in the world ever possessed you to leave the ball with those hillbillies? Not just *one* hillbilly but *three* of them!" Ralph's face contorted with anger as he glared at his daughter.

"Why, Papa, Ramsey was right there and I only gave them a ride to their hotel since Jeremy and the others were so hateful to them. I was grateful to them. Michael Tolbert accosted me backstage and Mr. Ross and his friends drove him away."

"Did that scoundrel Tolbert hurt you?" Sudden concern filled Ralph's voice.

"No, Papa, he didn't hurt me." She looked up at her father with a sad face, her eyes moist with tears. That usually got to him, and sure enough, it worked again. Ralph sputtered a few more choice, angry words about the situation. It sounded like he was saying something about how he was glad they were there to help her when she needed it, but he was amazed at her thoughtlessness of taking off with three strange young men that she had never seen before. Finally, shrugging his shoulders in disgust, he sat down in front of the fireplace, with his pipe and the newspaper, and turned his back to his rebellious daughter.

Elaine breathed a sigh of relief as her father's anger subsided, and she heard him mutter something about "hope you use better judgment next time."

Elaine tried to take on an air of indifference, but Nanny knew her too well. "Dat gal is up to sompin' and dat's a fac'!" After that, any time they were alone, Nanny pleaded with Elaine to confide in her, but she pretended innocence.

"Why, Nanny, you sweet old thing! It just makes me feel so good that you still worry about your little Missy, but honestly now, I have nothing to tell you!" Elaine climbed into bed and Nanny tucked the covers in around her as she had done all her life.

"Missy, you kin say whut you wants, but Ah knows you, an' Ah says you is up to no good!"

"Oh, Nanny, dear, please run away now so I can sleep! There's a love. Good night!" And rolling over with her back to the old servant, Elaine closed her eyes. As Nanny went over to put out the lamp, Elaine could hear her mumbling to herself. "Dat chile gonna git herself in a heap o' trouble or my name ain't Nanny!"

A little more than a month had passed since Elaine had come to the rescue of the three young men at the Debutante's Ball. Elaine went to the stables where she found her mare, Blaze, saddled and ready for her daily ride. As she mounted up, she didn't notice Nanny in a whispered conversation with Ramsey.

"Now, listen to whut Ah says, you lazy, good-fer-nothin' fiel' han'——"

"I ain't no fiel' han', Nanny, I's a yahd and stable han'!" Ramsey protested indignantly.

Nanny took hold of his shoulders and shook him like a rag doll. "Ah said, *listen*!. Now, listen! When young Missy go fer her ride, you foller her. See whur she go, and see whut she do, and mostly, see *who* she see! If'n you does this fer ol' Nanny, Ah'll bakes you a apple pie."

At the mention of apple pie, Ramsey grinned a big toothy grin, it's splendor diminished only slightly by a missing front tooth. "Yas'm, Nanny, I reckin' I could glide along right quietlike behind young Missy and finds out all dat fer you." Nanny nodded and slipped back into the house.

Unseasonable cold had settled over the city, and the broad expanse of the Mississippi looked slate gray under the overcast sky. Elaine found the cold invigorating as she galloped easily along the familiar path. She rounded a bend and rode back into a sheltered cove. Her face lit up as she saw the one waiting for her.

She slipped from her horse into Lonnie's waiting arms. "How long have you been waiting, dearest?" she asked as she snuggled next to his chest for warmth.

"Oh, not long."

"I try ta take a different way each time so no one will get suspicious," Elaine told him.

Suddenly, roughly, he took her by the shoulders and held her at arm's length. "Elaine, how long are we going to keep playing this hide and seek game?" Pain and frustration was etched deeply into his rugged young face. "Do ya have any idea how it makes me feel ta be sneakin' around like a polecat in a hen house jist ta see the girl I love fer a half hour?"

Unexpected shame engulfed Elaine. She hung her head. "I know, Lonnie, and I don't like it any better than—"

"Then let's *do* somethin' about it!" he cut in, frustration making his voice sharp.

"W-what do you mean?" she gulped, looking up into those wonderful blue eyes.

He cupped her chin with his hand and kissed her softly. "I want ta marry you, sweetheart. I want ta walk into the front door of yore house and shake yore daddy's hand like a man. I want ta take you to Oregon with me—ta build ourselves a new life in a new place." He pulled her closer. "I know I ain't no great catch. I ain't got the schoolin' like all yore friends and I cain't talk proper and all that. But I love you so much I hurt, honey." His blue eyes locked into hers. "It'll be lots a' hard work. We both know that. I won't be able ta give you what yore used to, neither, not right away anyhow. But we'll have a whole lifetime ta build our own fortune together."

Lonnie had to stoop to hear her answer; her voice almost a whisper. "Oh, Lonnie, I want to say yes, and I don't care about your lack of schooling, but I'm just barely eighteen years old, and—oh! I don't know! I just have to have more time to think about it!" she said miserably.

Evenly, Lonnie said, "Take all the time ya need to think it over, honey, but just remember this—one month from today, I'm leavin'. I'm goin' West—with ya or without cha. It's yore choice."

Before Elaine could speak, they both whirled toward the soft nicker of a horse close by.

Putting his finger to his lips, Lonnie took hold of her hand, and quietly they walked to the heavy underbrush that surrounded their secret rendezvous. Lonnie thrust back a clump of bushes, and there sat Ramsey, his eyes the size of silver dollars.

Upon being discovered he uttered a plaintive "Oh, Lawd, have mercy on dis man!"

With a jerk of the reins he tried to ride off, but Lonnie quickly grabbed the bridle and pulled him up short.

"Ramsey, what in the world are you doing out here? Why are you spying on us? Who put you up to this?" demanded Elaine angrily.

"It were dat Nanny, shores de worl', Missy. She done tole me to ride out after you and see whur you is and whut you is doin' and mostest of all she want to know *who* is you wif!" wailed Ramsey, shifting the blame guiltily from himself to Nanny.

His eyes were wide with fear, for although the Dentons had always been kind to him, there was always a first time for everything. He sure didn't want to be known as the first Denton slave to ever get a whipping! "Missy, I ain't goin' to git no whuppin' over dis hyar, am I?" Ramsey couldn't help asking, his heart in his mouth.

Elaine's own mouth dropped open at the very idea. "Well, for heaven's sake, Ramsey, of course you won't get a whipping! What a thing to say! You know Papa doesn't do that sort of thing!" Then more kindly she said, "Get along home now. Just tell Nanny you couldn't find me, you hear?"

"Yas'm, Missy, I is goin' right dis minute an' ah won't tell Nanny nuffin', naw, sir, Missy!" And a much relieved Ramsey took off for the Denton home as though the devil himself was after him!

Elaine and Lonnie looked at each other for a long moment. They both knew Ramsey would tell all as soon as Nanny got hold of him and they also knew that a big change was about to take place in their relationship. "I'll come home with ya and explain things ta your father," said Lonnie quietly.

Grimly, Elaine shook her head. "No, I'd better handle this myself."

"When will I see ya again?" he asked, catching her two small hands in his big, strong ones.

"In a few days, maybe. I don't know what my parents will do when they find out about my meeting you like this."

Sadly, he leaned down and touched his lips to hers, thinking this could be the last time he'd ever see her. "I wish you had let me call on ya at yore house in the proper way like I wanted to in the first place. Then we wouldn't be in this mess."

"I know you wanted to, and I *wanted* you to, but the way Mama and Papa feel about things I just felt it to be an impossible situation." Big tears welled up in her eyes.

"Go on home now, Honey," Lonnie said gently. "Remember our talk here this afternoon. I'll be back here tomorrow. Meet me if ya can. If yore not here, I'll know what yore answer is."

As he helped her onto her horse, Elaine touched his cheek. "I do love you, you know."

"I know."

CHAPTER 7

THE CLOCK ON THE MANTLE ticked loudly in the silence of Ralph Denton's study. Ralph sat behind the big desk, his brow a thundercloud. Blanche reclined on the sofa, dabbing her eyes, and occasionally taking a whiff of smelling salts. Elaine sat in a high-backed chair, ramrod straight, face noncommittal, her eyes dry. Nanny stood directly behind Elaine's chair, twisting her apron, her mouth set firmly. The tension was so thick you could have cut it with a knife.

"Well, young lady, we're waiting for an explanation," growled Ralph, glaring at his daughter.

"Ah *tole* you whur she wuz, Marse Ralph! She wuz out in a hidey-hole wid dat no-count, pore white trash!" declared Nanny indignantly. "Ah tole—"

"Nanny," barked Ralph, his voice ringing with authority. "I'm speaking to my daughter!" Nanny's mouth shut with a snap, and she stood glaring at him, taking license with her age and her position with the family.

"Elaine, dahlin', please give your father a plausible explanation for the things Nanny has told us," begged Blanche from the depths of the sofa.

Suddenly, everything fell into place for Elaine. She knew what her explanation must be. "All right, Mama, but neither you nor Papa will like what I'm going to say." With a sudden lightness of heart and spirit, she faced her father. "I met Lonnie Ross at the cove every day for the past few weeks because I knew you and Mama wouldn't receive him here at the house."

She met the thundercloud in her father's eyes squarely. "I've come to know his goodness and his kind heart." With her every word, her parents were sitting up straighter, unable to believe what they were hearing.

"This afternoon he asked me to marry him and travel west to homestead in Oregon."

Ralph's fist slammed down onto the desk, sending papers and ledgers flying. "Oregon! Oregon? I will not allow any daughter of mine—!"

Quickly Elaine rose to her feet, meeting her father's anger head on. "It's no use, Papa. This afternoon I couldn't give him an answer, but now I realize if I let him go west by himself, part of me would be lost forever." She leaned forward and put her hands on the desk. "I love him, Papa, and I'm going to marry him whether you and Mama give me your blessing or not." She went over and put her arms around her mother who looked as though she was about to faint for real this time. She kissed her cheek. "I'm going up to my room now, Mama. You and Papa can talk over what I've said. I'd love for you to help me with my wedding plans, and I do so want my Papa to give me away, but if you can't accept Lonnie into your home and into our family, then we'll elope, and you will lose me forever. I love you both," she said, her voice very soft. "Please understand." As she left the room both of her parents were begging her to sit down and discuss it further. Elaine kept walking.

That evening as she climbed into her beautiful bed and pulled up the soft sheets, her mother knocked on the door. "Dahlin', may I come in?" she asked softly.

"Yes, Mama, come on in."

Her mother came over and sat down on the edge of the bed, looking down at the daughter she loved more than life itself, trying to figure out a way to explain something to her that she didn't fully understand herself. "I want to talk to you about Trixie," she said, wincing at the look on Elaine's face.

"All right. Go ahead," she said, steeling herself for she knew not what.

"We bought Imogene shortly after we built the house. She was the next slave we bought after Nanny. It is very difficult for me to speak to you of these things." Blanche's voice was so soft that Elaine had to strain to hear her. Fanning herself vigorously, Blanche continued. "It is common for a master to have children with his female slaves." Elaine started to speak but Blanche cut her short. "No, dahlin', please let me get this out. This is very difficult for me. It is something that is done and everyone knows it, but no one talks about it. You deserve to know the truth, no matter how hard it is for your Papa and I to face."

"Your father and I were young and I was carrying you. I wasn't feeling well a lot of the time and well, Imogene was young back then, too. He did what a lot of red-blooded slave owners have done for years. And I must be honest, dahlin', I really didn't mind so much and—"

"Didn't *mind*!" exclaimed Elaine. "You didn't *mind*! How can that be? You were his wife and he committed adultery with a slave. They had a child! How could you not *mind*?" Elaine burst into tears and turned her back to her mother, every fiber of her being raging at the incredible story her mother was revealing.

"Dahlin', I don't expect you to understand, but please know that your father and I are happy and have always been for the most part. Our marriage is good and we love each other very much." Blanche put her hand on her daughter's shoulder. "Please don't hate us. Things seemed different back then." Blanche's voice became tight with emotion and embarrassment. "It's very difficult to talk to you about this but you're about to be married and move far away from us. I feel I must make you understand." Blanche placed a delicate hand on Elaine's shoulder and gently turned her back over to face her. "I was raised that ladies do not enjoy the physical side of marriage. We were to endure it to provide our husbands with children. Female slave women have always lifted that particular burden from the wife. We didn't think you'd ever know about Trixie. We should have told you. I know that now and I am so sorry for the way you found out. It must have been dreadful for you."

"I don't hate you and Papa," she said slowly, "but I don't think I can ever understand." Blanche embraced her daughter, holding her close for a very long time, then walked slowly and sadly out of the room.

The next day, Lonnie found Elaine waiting for him as he rode into the cove. He took one look at her radiant face and the love in her eyes, and he pulled her down from her horse and kissed her until she was breathless! "I can't cook!" she mumbled against his lips. "I don't care!" he said, kissing her again. "I don't know how to do laundry!" and again Lonnie replied with an "I don't care!" and a kiss. They laughed as only young people in love can. "Come home with me now, Lonnie. My parents are waiting to meet you."

Ralph and Blanche knew their daughter and knew she meant what she said about marrying this boy and going to Oregon, but they hoped to be able to change Lonnie's mind and convince him to stay in St. Louis. Ralph was willing to offer him a good position in his business. They would be well set.

Elaine would never forget that first meeting between her parents and Lonnie. She felt so ashamed of herself that she had hidden her relationship with this good man from them. He walked in with his head held high, shook Ralph's hand and removed his hat as he spoke to Blanche. He took the seat that was offered to him and Elaine would always remember his words. "First of all, Mr. Denton, I want ta apologize fer sneakin' around behind yore back ta see yore daughter. I want ya to know straight out that it was not my idea ta do it that way." Ralph and Blanche both looked at Elaine. They understood what he was telling them.

"Mr. Ross, I'll be quite honest with you. Her mother and I don't like this whole thing one bit. However, you seem to be an honorable young man with high ambition, and my daughter tells us she is determined to marry you. So I have a proposal to make you."

Elaine stared at her father, not knowing where he was going with this line of thought.

"As you know, Denton Enterprises owns several warehouses. We're always shorthanded and I'm looking for a good man to run them for us. Someone who can handle themselves and slow up the turnaround in the workforce down there. How about it, son? You and Elaine won't have to go traipsing off to Oregon or wherever it is you're talking about. You can stay right here in St. Louis and make her a fine living."

Lonnie cleared his throat uncomfortably, taking some time before he answered. "Sir, I thank ya kindly fer the offer. It sounds like it would be a real good way ta make a livin', but I ain't cut out ta run no warehouse. I'm used ta bein' outdoors. I'd never make it."

Blanche reached out and rested her hand on Lonnie's arm. "Mr. Ross—" she began.

"Lonnie, please, ma'am," said Lonnie quickly.

"Lonnie, look around you. Can't you see what our daughter is used to? She's never wanted for anything a day in her life. Do you think she would even last out the trip to Oregon, let alone the brutal hardships you're offering her at the end of the trail?" By now tears were flowing freely down Blanche's cheeks.

"Mama," broke in Elaine, "Have you ever known me to fail at anything I set my mind to do?"

Weakly, Blanche smiled. "Well, dahlin', I have to say I have not."

"I love Lonnie. I want to be his wife, bear his children. I cannot bear to think of life without him. Can't you understand?"

Lonnie stood and put his arm around Elaine and faced her parents. "Sir, Elaine and I love each other and we want ta be married. I'll take real good care 'a her, Mr. Denton, I promise ya that. I know I don't have a lot 'a schoolin' and I shore ain't got much money, but we're both young and strong. Oregon is a land 'a plenty where a man can grow corn taller than two men. There's land for the takin' out there, good rich fertile land. Together we're gonna make a real nice home fer ourselves, out there in a place that most men just dream of!" His eyes were shining as he described his dream to Elaine's father.

In spite of himself, Ralph felt moved by Lonnie's earnestness and his genuine love for his daughter. "You've known each other such a short time," he said quietly.

"I don't know how you feel about love at first sight, sir, but that's what happened to us." Elaine was nodding in agreement.

Silently, Ralph stood, laid his hand on Lonnie's shoulder, and left the room shaking his head. He knew he'd been bested.

Blanche took a good hard look at her daughter and thought sadly that Elaine had become a woman and she hadn't even noticed.

The next day, Elaine rose up early and went down to the kitchen where Imogene busied about, preparing breakfast. She wasn't greeted with the usual big smile and a "Good mawnin' to ya, Missy!" and Elaine knew that she was ill at ease. Even in a house as large as the Denton mansion, there were no secrets. The servants always knew everything going on in the house and she knew that Imogene was very aware of the conversation between Blanche and herself last night. She went over to Imogene and touched her shoulder. "Imogene, it's okay. Mama and I had a good talk last night. I'll admit I don't understand it, but it explains a lot of things. I always felt close to Trixie. We were inseparable as children. I also understand now why she has grown to resent me. I am leading a life she was never allowed to lead."

Imogene looked at her young mistress, seeing a wisdom far beyond her years. "Yas'm, dat's true, I reckon. Ah's mighty glad you don' hold it agin' me." A big tear slowly trickled down her cheek. "Marse Ralph allus been good to me 'n' my girl, ya know."

"Didn't you resent being used, Imogene? How did it make you feel?" Elaine asked.

Imogene thought for a long moment before she answered. "Well, Missy, to tells you de truf, dem kinda thoughts never entered ma head. Ah jist done whut Ah was tol'. It were a big honor that

Marse Ralsph chose me," she said, looking to see how Elaine was taking this.

"I don't pretend to understand, Imogene, but I'm trying." Elaine reached out and took a work-worn hand in her own soft one. "Actually, I came down here this morning to ask your help with something very important."

"Whut kin Ah do fer ya, Missy?"

"Do you think you can teach me to make those big biscuits like you do?" she asked with a smile.

"We'll shore gives it a try!" replied Imogene. Instantly, the air was cleared of all uncomfortableness and it was just like old times. She handed Elaine a big apron to protect her dress and they began her first cooking lesson. In a few moments, Trixie came in.

"Well, well, If it ain't my long lost sistah!" she said in a mocking tone.

"Trixie! You 'pologize to Missy right now!" scolded Imogene.

"Why should I has to 'pologize fer de truth, Mammy?" she said, staring at Elaine coldly. "After all, we is sistahs, now ain't we?"

Elaine wiped the flour from her hands and went over to face Trixie. Softly she said, "Trixie, I loved you like a sister, when we were little. Then we grew up and weren't allowed to do things together anymore just because of 'the way things were.' I know you have a lot of anger and resentment toward me and I'm so sorry. I just didn't know."

Trixie burst into tears and left the room. She ran out to the stables, searching frantically from stall to stall until at last she saw him—Jessie—the love of her life. Broad-shouldered, gleaming black skin and his kind face looking very concerned as Trixie came bursting in.

"Trixie, Honey! Whut's wrong?" Jessie asked, taking her shaking body into his arms.

"Oh, Jessie, I'm just so mixed up! Missy is trying to get me to be with her like I used to when we were kids, but I just can't! I'm scared too. I don't know what will happen to me now that Missy knows about Mammy and Marse Ralph." Jessie could see the fear in her eyes.

"Well, Ah tells you whut! Ah been hearin' about dese here wagon trains dey calls 'em. Dey takes folks 'way off to a place called Californ-y and lotsa other places. Dey say dere's somethin' out dere called de ocean. Water out as fer as ya kin see and den some! Ah been thinkin' Ah might jist slip off from dis here place 'n' hitch a ride on one o' dem wagaon trains." Gently, Jessie took her by the shoulders and moved her back to where he could see her face. "How 'bout you and me takin' off together and catchin' one o' dem trains, huh? We kin git married and start ourselves a whole new life, whur we wouldn't be beholden to any man. We'd be free, Honey!" His eyes bore into hers. "Well, whatcha think 'bout dat?"

Trixie didn't waste a moment in giving him her answer. "Oh, Jessie! I think that's a real good idea and I'd be proud to be your wife." They sealed their bargain with a tender kiss.

CHAPTER 8

Elaine Denton's engagement to the rugged young Illinois farmer set the St. Louis society a-buzzing! The house filled with callers, day after day, most saying they were there to congratulate her, but usually they ended up trying to talk her out of it. Finally, Elaine grew tired of the stream of well-meaning but meddlesome friends and acquaintances and simply refused to accept any callers. She left it up to her mother to deal with as well as most of the wedding plans.

Besides, she really didn't have time for all the socializing. Within two weeks, she must learn the basics of cooking and cleaning from the capable servants in her parent's household, for there would be no servants where she was going. Ralph had offered Lonnie two young slaves as a wedding gift, a man and a woman of his choice, but he politely, but firmly, refused.

"I know there's a lotta things ya don't like about me, Mr. Denton," said the honest young man to his future father-in-law," and ya'll just have ta add this to the list, I reckon. I appreciate whut yore tryin' ta do fer Elaine and me, but I ain't never owned another human bein', and I don't aim ta start now."

Ralph tried to protest, but Lonnie stood his ground. The older man just shook his head. He'd never understand this stubborn young man who had won his daughter's heart, but the boy had earned his grudging respect.

Elaine's wedding day broke bright and clear. She awoke earlier than usual, before Nanny even had a chance to come in to shake her awake as she normally did. She snuggled into her pillow and thought about the day ahead. She glanced at the clock on the mantle. Seven a.m. In seven hours, she would become Mrs. Lonnie Albert Ross! Her heart beat rapidly with anticipation.

Her friends thought she had lost her mind and maybe she had! But she knew that she couldn't stand to live without seeing those big blue eyes again. She also knew that her easy style of life as a spoiled little rich girl would end abruptly after the honeymoon. She knew it would be the most difficult thing she had ever done in her life, but she was excited about the trip and determined to make Lonnie a good wife.

Nanny came in and gently took hold of Elaine's shoulder. With a gentle shake she said, "Chil', it's time to git up. We's got to git you ready fo' yo' weddin' t'day," she finished brokenly. She had never completely accepted the marriage and the coming separation from the girl she had raised since the day she was born. Nanny would have given anything to be able to go with them, but she knew she was too old and could never stand the trip.

Elaine rolled over and took the old black woman's hands. "Oh, Nanny, I shall miss you more than Mama, I think. Please, don't cry, dear. Listen, I have a surprise for you!" Nimbly she hopped out of bed and went to a desk over beside the window. She removed a large single sheet of paper. "Do you know what this is, Nanny?"

"Well, 'course Ah know's whut dat is! It's a piece o' paper, Missy!" snapped Nanny indignantly, remembering practical jokes played on her in the past by her impudent young charge.

"Silly goose!" Elaine giggled. "Of course it's a piece of paper, but do you know what it says?"

"Missy, you knows us black folks ain't 'lowed to read writin'!"

Going over to her faithful old servant of eighteen years, Elaine took the rough, calloused hand in her own small soft one, and led her to a rocker in the corner.

As a child she had spent many happy hours on Nanny's lap in that rocker. "Sit down, Nanny, dear. This is the surprise I told you about. It's a gift from Lonnie and me, to you." Elaine sat down on the floor in front of her.

At the word *gift*, Nanny's eyes widened and she smiled in anticipation. "Well, land sakes, chil', tell ol' Nanny whut it is a-fore Ah plum es-splodes!"

Elaine had to smile at Nanny's childlike excitement. "Do you remember, Nanny, the stories you used to tell me while we rocked and rocked in that old chair?"

Nanny smiled and nodded, memories flooding her mind, distracting her from the promised surprise momentarily. "You wuz a mis-cheev-i-ous one, Missy, and dat's a fac'! You gimme a turn more'n onct, I reckon!"

"I remember when I had the measles. You and Mama took turns sitting up with me until my fever broke. You both looked so worried but I wasn't scared a bit. I heard you praying and I just knew God was watching over me. You've always made Him so real to me, Nanny."

"He shorely wuz in dis room, right by yore side ever' minute. Jes' remember, chil', de good Lawd loves and keeps dem dat call on His Name," Nanny replied. Anxious to get to the business at hand, she added, "Now, whut 'bout dis here gift you is talkin' 'bout?"

"I'm going to give you this gift because I love you, Nanny. This paper says you are free. *free*, Nanny!! You don't belong to Papa and Mama or me anymore! You don't belong to anyone! You are *free*!!"

"Free?" Nanny repeated the word softly, reverently. Silent tears of joy began to course down Nanny's leathery old cheeks as the reality of it started to sink in.

Elaine continued. "Papa says you can stay right here for the rest of your life. You can work if you want to or just sit and rock in that old rocking chair. It's all up to you now because you're free, Nanny!" Elaine leaned down and put her cheek lovingly up against the wet black one.

"Ah duzzin' know whut to say, Missy, I purely don'. Jes' thankee from de bottom o' dis ol' woman's heart."

"You don't have to thank me, Nanny. I want to do it. Besides, it was Lonnie's idea." She laid her soft white hands on Nanny's hardened black ones and gave them a squeeze. "Nanny, I've come to understand that it's wrong to own human beings. Color shouldn't make any difference. Since I found out about Trixie, I've changed my mind about a lot of things." Nanny patted her on the arm. "Lonnie is dead set against slavery and I've come to agree with him. I promise you, Nanny, we will never own a slave."

Nanny slowly processed the fact that it was Lonnie's idea to set her free and in spite of herself, she felt her heart soften toward the young stranger who was going to take her Missy from her. Lovingly, she caressed Elaine's cheek.

CHAPTER 9

THE VIEW DOWN THE CENTER aisle of the church was an imposing one. Elaine and her family had attended services here ever since she could remember. The ceiling towered with twelve huge chandeliers hanging down from the crossbeams at the peak. All the candles were lit for this special occasion. Multicolored lilies and roses decorated the altar area and huge bows in light blue and pale yellow adorned each pew down the center aisle. Large candelabras were on either side of the altar, with blue and yellow streamers hanging from them. The sun shone brightly through the elaborate stained-glass windows, giving the whole room a soft glow.

The pastor, in his black robe, stood patiently at the front. The guests, in their best attire, were smiling and whispering, while craning their necks toward the heavy wooden doors at the back of the church, waiting for the bride to make her appearance. A huge organ took up much of the left side of the sanctuary at the front by the altar. A prissy little man in a black suit adorned with a frilly white cravat and a yellow rose in his lapel waited for his cue to begin playing.

Elaine's knees felt so weak and shaky she thought she might collapse. She could see Lonnie and his two friends waiting at the altar. (They were the same two friends she had met at the Debutante Ball, Matthew Jones and Billie Thompson.)

Three of her six bridesmaids were adorned in pale blue gowns, and three wearing pale yellow gowns. All wore broad-brimmed hats with matching hatbands. Excitedly, they were chatting with the maid of honor, Amanda Hathcock. Amanda's gown was a lovely yellow and blue print, and adorning her broad-brimmed yellow hat was a hatband matching her gown. Her ring bearer and flower girl were the adorable children of family friends, the Thornton's. They were chasing each other and scuffling as little children do, sending their mother into a tizzy as she tried to calm them down and protect their good clothes.

Papa came up beside Elaine, taking her cold, nervous hands into his big warm ones. "You look so beautiful, Lainey," he told her, reverting to the nickname he had called her as a child. "You look so grown up." Tears welled up in his eyes. "It seems you've become a woman overnight!"

"Thank you, Papa," she said with a big hug. "You and Mama taught me well." Elaine smiled at her father.

He looked at her intently. "I want—no, I *need*—to apologize to you for my reaction to your young man." Elaine's protests were silenced by Ralph's fingers on her lips. "No, let me finish. Your mother and I were married and have lived our lives as we have pleased. Not always doing the right thing, but we worked together and love each other more today than ever. You and your Lonnie deserve the opportunity to do the same."

"Oh, Papa! I do love you so!" breathed Elaine as she threw her arms around her father giving him a big hug. They both felt the barrier that had been between them come down for good at that very moment.

Tears flowed down Ralph's cheeks. "One more thing, honey. About Trixie—

"Oh, Papa, you don't have to explain. Mama already told me all about it," Elaine interrupted.

"I know, but I need you to know that I will take care of Trixie. I promise you that."

"You'll free her?"

"Yes," he said simply. "I want to share something with you, honey. When you found out about Trixie, I couldn't bear the look of disappointment and shame that you gave me. I'll never forget thinking that you must hate me." A tear slowly made its way down her father's cheek. "I talked to Nanny. She has more sense in her little finger than most people, black or white, have in their whole body." Ralph smiled down at his daughter.

She returned his smile, wondering where his story was leading. "She told me that I would never feel right about anything until I got right with the Lord. I asked her to tell me how to do that and she did. Elaine, I've been saved, and I feel like a new man!"

She grabbed her emotional father and hugged him. "Oh, Papa, I can't believe it! I'm so glad. Nanny introduced me to Jesus when I was little and He helps me to be a better person than I could ever be on my own."

"It'll be a hard row to hoe, but I intend to free all the blacks right away. God has shown me that what Lonnie says is true. They're real people just like us."

Not believing her ears, Elaine placed her hand on her father's cheek. "Thank you," she said simply.

Blanche came up to them with tears flowing. "Oh, my precious girl, I just don't believe you're really going through with this!"

Her father broke in before she had a chance to reply, much to her surprise. "My dear, please get control of yourself. Elaine has made her decision and all the tears and pleading in the world won't change it. It will just drive a wedge between the two of you."

As though a switch were thrown, the tears stopped. Blanche delicately dabbed at her nose and carefully wiped away all signs of tears with her lace handkerchief. She pulled Elaine close—her one and only child whom she loved more than life itself. It terrified her to think of what lay ahead for her daughter—hardship, deprivation, Indian attacks! Blanche couldn't allow herself to think about it. "Are you ready, dahlin'?" she asked, resigning herself to the inevitable.

"Yes, Mama, I'm ready!" Elaine quickly gave her mother a big hug as the usher (Jeremy Craig) came to escort Blanche into the church.

He seated Blanche and the pastor nodded to the little man at the organ. As he began to play, little Thomas and Sarah started down the long aisle, just as they had practiced, dropping rose petals every so often. They were followed by her bridesmaids, with Amanda waiting her turn at the door. Elaine quickly hugged her lifelong friend and whispered, "Maybe someday soon you'll be the bride and Jeremy will be the groom!"

Amanda blushed but whispered back, "Maybe so! He's calling on me pretty often now."

Then it was her turn. The solemn strains of the wedding march filled the church as she started down that long aisle on her father's arm. As the guests rose, her eyes met Lonnie's, and all her nervousness left her as she joined him at the altar.

CHAPTER 10

Nanny carefully packed the trunks and boxes that the young couple would be taking with them to their new home in Oregon. Quilts and blankets, kitchen items, dishes, and a few pieces of furniture. Nanny insisted on Elaine taking the rocking chair. A thick cookbook that Mama gave her was tucked in with care. That cookbook held all the delicious family recipes Elaine had eaten all her life; wonderful Creole cuisine from Mama's family and the more traditional recipes from Papa's side. There were also helpful hints Mama had written in the margins that told her how many pints make a quart, how many teaspoons make a tablespoon, and how to make sour milk if you don't have buttermilk. They would be purchasing their food supplies in Independence just before starting their long trek west.

As she packed, Nanny's heart broke a little more. Each item was baptized with tears from the heartsick old servant. Ramsey was waiting for each container as Nanny sealed it. He carried them down to the stable where Lonnie placed them carefully into the wagon.

Elaine checked off each item as it was packed away. She racked her brain for anything else they might need, but could think of nothing. As she sat and watched her beloved Nanny, carefully placing their belongings into each container, she suddenly realized that Nanny didn't look well.

"Nanny, you look tired. Why don't we get Imogene to come up and help you?" Elaine said, concern in her voice.

"I ain't tard," answered the old woman crossly. "Anyways, washin' and arnin' all dese duds might make a body tard. No, ma'am! Little Missy! Ain't nobody else gonna pack my Missy's things," said Nanny, her jaw set stubbornly in a way with which Elaine knew all too well.

"Why not?" Elaine pleaded. "You could stay right here and make sure she does it right."

Nanny didn't answer but her silence spoke volumes to Elaine. "All right! All right!" Elaine conceded defeat. "I'm going down to the stable to see how Lonnie and Ramsey are coming with the wagon."

Nanny grunted noncommittally.

A shadow moved among the thick trees that surrounded the Denton estate, getting closer to the stables.

Elaine peered into the wagon, unable to believe the amount of boxes, trunks, and cartons that it held. She looked around for Lonnie, but the stable was silent except for the soft rustle of hay or an occasional nicker from the horses in the stalls at the other end.

The shadow moved from the trees and slipped into the stable without making a sound. Slowly, quietly, the shadow closed the distance separating it from the unsuspecting girl.

Elaine felt a hand on her arm. She turned with a smile expecting to see Lonnie. But it wasn't Lonnie. It was Michael Tolbert, looking haggard and obviously drunk. "Michael!" she gasped. "What are you doing here?"

"I had to see you," he replied, woodenly, his words slightly slurring as he spoke. Elaine could smell liquor on his breath and she was suddenly very conscious that they were alone in the stable.

"I love you, Elaine." She started to protest, but he cut her off. "Please hear me out," he begged. "I've been watching your house for days, trying to get a moment alone with you. Please listen to me." The desperation in his voice frightened her.

Horrified, she interrupted him. "Michael, I'm married! I love my husband very much and we're going to leave very soon."

"Forget him, Elaine!" He grabbed both her arms and pulled her up close to him. "I've wanted you ever since the first time I saw you. Leave that yokel and come away with me. I've got enough money so we could live like royalty for the rest of our lives. I can give you anything money can buy." He pulled her up against him and tried to kiss her. She twisted her head away from the kiss, but for just one brief moment Elaine compared the life to which she was accustomed to the stark poverty she knew she'd be facing with Lonnie. She compared this drunken dandy to her strong handsome Lonnie. Michael could never measure up. Not in a thousand years! Desperately, she struggled, trying to break fee of his grasp.

Suddenly, Lonnie's voice cut through the air like a steel blade. "You'll be turnin' loose'a my wife, I reckon." His voice was low, almost a growl.

Michael turned her loose so quickly she stumbled, almost falling. He drunkenly groped into his coat and she screamed as he pulled out a gun. Lonnie pounced on him in a flash, knocking the gun from his hand, then planting a solid blow to his jaw, sending him sprawling into a pile of horse manure and straw. Lonnie turned to his shaken bride. "Are you okay, honey? Do you want me to get the constable?"

Numbly, Elaine shook her head. "N-no, no, I'm fine. Just make him leave, please," she answered, visibly shaken.

Lonnie removed the bullets from the gun and handed it back to the intruder. "Get out and don't you ever come near my wife again! Do you understand me?"

Michael stood up, rubbing his jaw. He returned the gun to his jacket, then picked his hat up off the floor, flicking off a chunk of manure that clung to it. Then very deliberately, he placed it on his head, touched the brim toward Elaine with a mock bow and without a word disappeared into the darkness.

Lonnie rushed to her side, sweeping her shaking body into his arms. Kissing her tear-stained face, he murmured words of love and consolation until she relaxed.

"He's out of his mind, Lonnie," she said when she finally got control of herself. "He actually wanted me to leave you and run away with him. He was drunk! Falling down drunk!" And she began to cry again.

"I swear if he ever comes near you again, I'll kill 'im with my bare hands!" Elaine had no doubt that her husband was dead serious.

"Well, dearest, in a few days we won't have to worry about him anymore." With determination, Elaine tried to put the whole incident out of her mind. She went back to the house and up the stairs. As she reached the door to her room, she screamed. Nanny lay very still, in a heap on the floor.

Elaine shook her and called her name repeatedly, but Nanny did not respond. She remembered running into the hallway, screaming for help. Mama had immediately taken charge of the situation, sending Ramsey to go fetch Dr. Martin. Ramsey had run out faster than Elaine could ever remember him moving in her whole life! He loved Nanny too.

When Dr. Martin arrived, he checked for a pulse or a heartbeat one more time, but to no avail. Sadly, he shook his head and slowly pulled up the white sheet to cover the lifeless black face.

Everyone in the room was crying, black and white alike. Nanny was the first house servant Ralph had purchased when he and Blanche were newlyweds. Her kindness, wit, and level head quickly earned her a place in the nursery when Elaine was born. She had been Elaine's servant, confidante, friend, and second mother ever since, and had been treated as one of the family. More importantly, she had led most of them to Jesus over the years, and they had looked to her for advice and spiritual guidance.

Poor Nanny! Everyone said she just died of a broken heart. She never got to enjoy her new freedom. In her mind's eye, Elaine could see Nanny's still figure lying on the bedroom floor.

CHAPTER 11

ELAINE'S BODY WAS ONE WRENCHING ache, from her head to her toes. Her hair and clothes were full of dust, as were her mouth and nostrils. She had never been so tired for even one day as she had been every day in the two months since they left Independence. However, she tried not to complain and never regretted her decision to marry her blue-eyed pioneer, not even for a second. She knew she was one of the lucky ones who got to ride if she chose. Most walked the entire two-thousand-mile trip because they had overloaded their wagons and there simply was no room to ride. She had been amazed at the debris along the trail as the travelers soon realized that they had to unload some items or they wouldn't make it to Oregon. Furniture, food, and various other things littered the trail.

They had traveled by steamboat from St. Louis to Independence, Missouri. There they had unloaded the wagon they had brought with them. It would be their home for the next four to six months as they joined a wagon train of sojourners such as themselves.

Lonnie had had a stroke of luck in finding a spot for them on the very first day with a train led by a man simply known to all as "Buck." This legendary wagon master had made a dozen trips from Independence to the Oregon country. Buck had been a mountain man much of his adult life, until the trickle of settlers traveling westward had become a raging stream and the life he had known slowly became a thing of the past. Now Buck, being a reasonable man, "figgered as to how if'n you cain't beat 'em, jine 'em!" In just a few trips he became one of the most sought-after wagon masters on the trail. Each time he returned to Independence, he found more and more people waiting to go to Oregon on the next wagon train.

Lonnie and Elaine bought enough food for their trip. Taking Buck's advice, they bought 200 pounds of flour, 150 pounds of bacon, 10 pounds of coffee, 20 pounds of sugar, and 10 pounds of salt. They also learned that the big, beautiful team of horses they brought would have to be traded for a more sturdy team of oxen. Buck told them nobody in their right minds drove horse-drawn wagons. The horses wouldn't last even halfway due to the ruggedness of the trail, according to him.

Finally came the day to begin their journey. Buck had told them, "When the prairie grass is high enough so's the livestock'll have enough ta eat on the trip, it'll be time ta head out fer Ory-gon!" As Lonnie and Elaine looked out across the prairie, they saw the grass rippling in the wind that blew constantly.

Buck cried out, "Wagons, ho!" and they started on the most grueling period of time Elaine had ever experienced in her short life. All the wagon trains were trying to go at the same time and a tremendous traffic jam resulted! There were accidents as inexperienced drivers tipped their wagons over, and some couldn't even get their oxen to move. Some were just going in circles, unable to make the oxen go forward. Slowly but surely everyone got straightened out. They were moving. They were on the way to Oregon!

Buck (no one knew his real name) had taken an immediate shine to Lonnie and his new bride. Lonnie's hard work and his willingness to help his neighbor impressed the old mountain man. It was "plum unusual" to see all those qualities in one so young, and a cheerful attitude to boot!

The old wagon master looked at the young Mrs. Ross hanging on for dear life on the lurching wagon seat, and an unsolicited feeling of sympathy for the plucky little rich gal from St. Louis washed over him. "Them two are jist bound to make it!" he thought to himself.

Elaine took a great deal of comfort in the fact that Buck rode nearby. The farther they went, the wilder the country seemed to be, and she rested easier when they circled up and made camp for the night, knowing the old man was there, always watching, always listening. She allowed her mind to wander back to St. Louis for a brief moment. She smiled again, with a blush, as she remembered their honeymoon.

Her parents had tried to give the newlyweds a short trip down the Mississippi as a wedding gift. They would have traveled in luxury down river to a quaint, private inn that catered to the very rich. There they would have spent their first week together, pampered, spoiled, playing all day long. Lonnie and Elaine both knew that the honeymoon trip was out of the question. There was just too much to do and so little time. Instead, they settled for a weekend at the Planter's Hotel. It was very nice and her father insisted on paying for the honeymoon suite.

After the reception, held in the very ballroom where they had first met, Lonnie and his new bride went up to the honeymoon suite. He had unlocked the door and gallantly swept her up in his strong arms, carrying her across the threshold. Elegance and beauty filled the room, but they could have cared less. They only had eyes for each other.

Elaine was amazed and grateful for Lonnie's gentleness as they fulfilled their love that night. Wrapped in each other's arms, she watched her new husband's face as he slept. Softly, she ran her fingers through his thick blond hair, smiling at how boyish he looked in sleep. His eyes opened and he smiled at her, pulling her closer and kissing her. "Well, Mrs. Ross, would ya like me ta ring room service ta bring us some breakfast?"

"Oh, that would be wonderful, Mr. Ross!" she returned in the same lighthearted manner. They had ordered their breakfast and ate ravenously. They spent the better part of the morning making love and talking about everything that came to mind. When you came right down to it, all they really knew about one another was the love they felt and they found it delightful as they discovered new things as they talked. Finally, Elaine broached the subject she had been avoiding. "Lonnie, th-there's something about me you don't know and I want to tell you about it," she said timidly.

"Honey, there ain't nothin' you can tell me that would make any difference in how I feel about ya. You know that, don'cha?" he asked, looking deep into her eyes. With a deep breath, Elaine said, "You know the light-skinned slave at our house? The cook's daughter, Trixie? She-she's my half-sister!" Elaine blurted the last out and started to cry.

Lonnie pulled her close, then cupped her chin in his big hand and kissed her softly, brushing the tears from her cheeks. "I know that, honey. I'd heard about it quite a while back, but yore Pa set me down and explained it ta me one day when you'n yore Ma was out doin' whatever it was you was doin' about the weddin'."

Somewhat taken aback, Elaine pulled back and looked at him. "You *heard* about it? Was I the only person in St. Louis who didn't know?" she asked incredulously.

"Maybe, but when all is said and done, what does it matter? Does it change anything? Not fer me it don't. I love you and I don't care if ya got a houn' dawg fer a sister!" He grinned as she swatted him on the shoulder.

"It really doesn't matter to you, does it, dearest?" Elaine looked at her husband with new eyes. This man she married was a real gem. She had never known anyone so genuine and without malice or prejudice.

"Not one bit!" Lonnie pulled her close again and grinned wickedly. "Now, I can think of a lot better things ta do than talk about yore sister." His kiss cut off any retort she might have been ready to give.

The wagon train circled up for the night. While Lonnie tended to the horses, Elaine carefully built a campfire as he had taught her and set about preparing their evening meal. Trixie and Jessie would have helped them with their chores, but Lonnie had told them to just enjoy their new-found freedom and he and Elaine would fend for themselves. They'd served the Denton family faithfully for years, now this was their time. Trixie had thrown her arms around her sister and squeezed hard. "Oh, Missy! Thank you! This is all just like a dream!". Trixie's smile said it all. Jessie put one big hand on Elaine's shoulder and wrung Lonnie's hand with the other. Holding hands, he and Trixie returned to their wagon, loving their wonderful new life! Her mind drifted back to the first night out on the trail and her face colored with embarrassment, even yet, to think of the spectacle she had made of herself! She had determined that just because she was on a dusty old wagon train, that she would still dress for dinner as her family always did back in St. Louis. So there she stood, in hoopskirts and ruffles galore, trying to cook dinner over a campfire, when someone shouted, "Yore on fire, lady! Git down on the ground and roll over!" Stupidly she had looked around to see what all the shouting was about. Suddenly she was knocked violently to the ground and someone began to roll her over and over, like a rolling pin. She heard a voice say, "Ya wanna burn ta death, ma'am? Yore dress was on fire and ya didn't even know it! Ya cain't wear them foderols out here on the trail. Ain't you got no reg'lar clothes?" Through eyes filled with scalding tears of embarrassment and fright she saw Buck sitting on the ground beside her.

Elaine gulped and mumbled, "Yes, I do."

More gently, he said, "Wal, then, ya better go change inta one of 'em. I reckon this'uns done fer!" He grinned and spat as he stood to help her to her feet. A small gathering of some of the other passengers was staring at her. Some were laughing.

Trixie came running over to her. "Oh, Missy! Are you alright? Just look at your pretty dress!" she said sympathetically.

"Yes, I'm fine, Trixie! It's my own stupid fault! I should have known better!" Elaine replied, humiliated.

Suddenly a very large lady stepped up to her and put her arm around Elaine's shoulders.

"There now, honey, don't you fret about these gawkers." Glaring at the bystanders, she went on, "I don't reckon they've got anything better to do than to stand around starin'!" Then more kindly she said, "My name's Thelma, Thelma Casey. What's yours?"

"Elaine Ross, ma'am. Pleased to meet you and thank you. I-I just don't know what to do out here like this. I've always lived in St. Louis, and I've never had to cook or build a campfire or—!" Elaine covered her face with her hands, her shoulders shaking.

Thelma Casey's red, work-worn hand patted Elaine's shoulder. "There, there, honey. Don't get all upset. It's okay. You stay close to me on this old trip and I'll help you all I can. Now, get yourself cleaned up, and from now on, you better leave them fru-fru dresses in the trunk. Wear something plain with as little as possible to stick out so's you don't catch on fire or get caught in a rolling wagon wheel." Thelma hugged Elaine like she was one of her many children and Elaine felt the tears well up again. What had she let herself in for? She thanked God for Thelma's kindness.

The hug reminded her of Nanny. She always consoled her with a big hug. It was still hard to believe Nanny was dead. They had buried her the day after she died, with all the pomp and circumstance that Nanny would have loved. They placed her in a fancy walnut coffin with red velvet lining. No plain pine box for their Nanny. Flowers filled the little Baptist church where Nanny had worshipped since the Dentons brought her to St. Louis. The choir sang in mournful dirge all of Nanny's favorite songs: "Swing Low, Sweet Chariot," "What a Friend," and "Amazing Grace." She was buried in the Negro cemetery under a big oak tree. A huge headstone adorned her grave. There were few headstones in the Negro cemetery. Most of the graves were just marked with rocks or wooden crosses. Nanny would have been very proud to see how the family honored her memory.

Sadness overwhelmed Elaine as she wiped the tears from her face and tiptoed in to check on Charla. The child was fast asleep, looking like a little angel.

Elaine went back to her bedroom and turned out the lamp. She tossed and turned, trying to go to sleep, but sleep was elusive this night. She got up and relit the lamp, once again picking up her journal. The memories crowded her mind and Elaine allowed them to flow over her.

The day before Lonnie and Elaine left home, Ralph called everyone in the household together into the large dining room. Elaine remembered that she and Lonnie, Mama, Imogene, and Trixie were seated at the table and the other servants were standing. "I suppose you all are wondering why I called you in here today," began Ralph in his very best authoritative voice. "Well, as you all know, tomorrow, Missus Elaine and Mr. Lonnie will be leaving for Oregon. Her mother and I wanted to give them a going-away present." He paused, and glanced over at Blanche, who nodded as if encouraging him to go on. He cleared his throat and began again. Pointing to Lonnie and Elaine, he said, "These young people have opened my eyes to something I could never see before. That is, how wrong it really is to own slaves."

Elaine gasped audibly and took hold of Lonnie's arm. He was actually going to go through with it! Ralph Denton was getting ready to hand freedom to every black person that he owned.

Ralph continued. "I'd like to set it right, beginning today." He picked up a stack of papers. "There is a paper here with each and every one of your names on it." He waved the papers around the room to indicate all were included. "You all are free men, women, and children." He paused and looked around the room for their reactions. Most were stupefied, open-mouthed incredulity on each face. Unable to take it all in, no one said anything. You could have heard a pin drop.

"Did you understand what I just said?" He looked at them each one, his gaze moving around the room. "You are all free. I would like to keep you working for me, however, if you want to. Anyone who would like to continue working for wages, just let me know. I want you all to be successful and I'll help you any way I can."

He walked over to Trixie and took her by the hand. She looked up at him, her eyes wide. She didn't know what to expect. All of this was too much to take in. "Trixie, I want to send you to school if you'd like to go and you will never want for anything. Your sister has asked that you become a real part of this family, and Missus Blanche and I intend to honor that request as best we can."

Trixie slowly turned her head to look first at her mother, then at Elaine. Big tears spilled out of her huge dark eyes. "Missy, you really asked Mister Ralph to do that for me?" she asked softly, dropping the slave jargon that she had been using recently.

Elaine nodded, tears in her own eyes. The girls stood up slowly, as though on cue, and embraced. "I'm glad you're my sister, Trixie. I've always loved you as though you were," Elaine said softly. She turned to Blanche. "Mama, can you do this?" Blanche nodded and smiled a sad smile.

"Wrongs were committed in lots of ways," said Blanche, "but Trixie had no part in any of it. She's been an innocent victim in this whole thing, and it was beyond Imogene's control as well. Your Papa and I would like to help them all we can."

Elaine's heart was heavy because she knew her mother and father's lives would change drastically from this day forward. Missouri was a split state on the issue of slavery, and she knew that Ralph would lose many business accounts over the fact that he had set his slaves free. She knew their social lives would probably grind to a halt. She felt such love and pride in them for the strength they were showing today.

Through all this, Imogene sat silent, looking around her as though everyone had lost his mind. "Ah don't understand, Missus. What 'bout me? What does Ah *do* if Ah'm free? Ah don't b'lieve Ah knows how to be free." Like the others, Imogene's face was filled with confusion.

Blanche laid a reassuring hand on Imogene's arm. "If you would like to continue to work for us as our cook and live-in maid, we will provide you with a fair wage and room and board. We want that very much if you would like to stay."

"Thankee, Missus. Ah'd sho like to stay. Dis hyar's my home too." Imogene smiled, relief all over her face.

Jessie stepped forward. He was a big, handsome young man, very strong, his muscles bulging from blacksmithing. He spoke up. "Marse Ralph?"

"Yes, Jessie," Ralph answered.

"Marse Ralph, Trixie and me, well, we be in love an' we'd sho like to git married. Kin we do dat?" He was crushing his hat in his hands in nervousness.

"Jessie, you're a free man and Trixie is a free woman. Trixie, do you love Jessie?"

"Yes, sir, I love him with all my heart," Trixie said breathlessly.

"And, Marse Ralph," Jessie added. "Since we is free, do dat mean we kin go any place we pleases?"

"That's right, Jessie, if that's what you want to do," answered Ralph.

"So if we'ns wants to, we kin go to dis here Ory-gon lak Missy and Mistah Lonnie gonna do?"

Trixie whirled around and looked hard at Jessie, then back to Ralph. Her eyes were shining with excitement. "Oh, could we?" she asked.

"If that's what you want to do, I can't stop you. You are free to do as you wish," Ralph said in resignation. Turning to Trixie, he asked, "Are you sure you don't want to stay here and attend school?"

"That's a wonderful thought, Mister Ralph, but Jessie and I have been in love for a long time. To be able to go to a new land, as free people, to start a new life on our own, and make our own way—!" She stopped talking, overcome by the emotion of the moment.

Elaine was clapping her hands and Lonnie rushed over and clasped Jessie's hand. "It'll be fine ta have people along that we know and trust," Lonnie told him. "If you all want to go with us, we'll put off our trip one more week to give you'ns a chance to git married and git yourselves outfitted ta go."

Jessie looked at Trixie and held out his arms. Trixie ran to him and they hugged and laughed. "We'll do jist dat, Mistah Lonnie. We be ready in a week!"

"I'll see to it you have everything you need," said Ralph. "It'll be my wedding present to you!"

Elaine ran to her father and threw her arms around him. "Oh, thank you, Papa! You're wonderful!"

Two days later, Trixie and Jessie were married in the Negro Baptist Church where they had attended their whole lives. Elaine and Lonnie stood up with them, and they took the surname of Denton, as slaves were usually just called by a given name. As freed individuals, they could now have last names, the same as white people. It was common for freed slaves to take the surname of their former masters and Ralph encouraged them to do so. He tried his best to talk them into staying on with them in St. Louis, but they had stars in their eyes as they planned their new life in Oregon.

CHAPTER 12

◦

DAY BROKE OVER THE MOUNTAINS with a splash of dusty rose that quickly became golden as the sun steadily pushed its way into the sky.

As Elaine and Lonnie prepared for the day's journey, she caught a glimpse of a thin young man talking to a group of Indians who had been following the wagon train begging for handouts. She sucked in her breath and shook her head incredulously, still not believing her eyes! It was Michael Tolbert, the same Michael Tolbert who had pleaded for her hand and had been rejected by a very different Elaine. (Had it only been four months ago? It seemed so much longer somehow.) The same Michael Tolbert who had drunkenly assaulted her in the stable on the night before they left. Why was he on this train? Why had she not seen him before? Had he followed her? She was terrified to think what might come of another encounter between Lonnie and Michael. What would Lonnie do when he found out Michael was on this train? She had to tell him. He would find out soon enough anyway. She found her husband working on a broken trace on the harness. "Lonnie, Michael Tolbert is on this train," she said quietly.

His reply surprised her. "Yeah, I know. He's been layin' pretty low. He's got a right ta be anywhere he wants ta be, I reckon. The only place he don't have a right ta be is anywhere near you." He went back to his work without another word. Elaine stared at him in disbelief. Would she ever understand her new husband?

During one of his less sober moments a day or two later, Michael had made a fool of himself and built a fire under Lonnie, by telling all those in earshot that he was on the wagon train for one reason only, Elaine Denton. Lonnie had reminded him, none too gently, that her name was Ross now, and that he would advise him not to forget it again. He also told him if he ever came near his wife again, he'd kill him. Michael had passed out before he could respond.

Elaine stayed as far away from Michael as she could. She felt a little sorry for him, but she was afraid someone would get seriously hurt or even killed if he and Lonnie tangled again.

A band of ragtag-looking Indians had been following the wagon train for days, begging for food and actually helping the settlers round up straying stock or lift wagons when wheels needed to be repaired. Unlike the tall tales they had heard before they left Independence, the Indians had been a nuisance at times but never were a cause for concern. They had really been very helpful at times.

Out of the corner of her eye, she saw Michael look furtively all around, then motioning for the Indians to come over to his wagon; he reached inside and produced a liquor jug. After taking a long pull on the jug himself, he passed it to the Indians, who by this time were all smiles.

Elaine watched, aghast at what she was seeing. Didn't Michael know he was breaking the law by giving those Indians whiskey? She touched Lonnie's elbow and motioned for him to watch what was taking place.

As the jug completed its round and came back to its owner, he took another healthy pull, replaced the cork, and started to return it to its former hiding place, but the Indians were having none of it! Smiles were gone now, replaced by menacing looks. One of the younger braves grabbed the jug from Michael's hand. A scuffle broke out, and before long, they were rolling around on the ground, still holding firmly to the jug.

By this time, several people from the wagon train had heard the commotion and had come to see what it was all about. None of the spectators, red or white, interfered with the two men struggling on the ground.

Suddenly, the jug struck a rock and broke into a dozen pieces. Quick as a cat, the young brave leapt to his feet, and as one person the people from the wagon train drew in their breath at the wicked-looking knife he now held. The other Indians showed no sign of emotion at the change in the timber of the fight.

Michael grabbed a jagged piece of the broken jug, and ever watchful, crouching low, they circled each other, each man looking for an opportunity to strike.

With lightning speed, the Indian lunged at Tolbert, and with a sweeping motion, the knife made a deep gash in the white man's arm. Tolbert dropped the jagged crockery he was holding and grabbed his arm. The Indian moved in for the kill, but Tolbert wasn't finished yet. He caught the brave's fist as the knife once again tried to make contact with his flesh. The struggle was becoming more and more violent.

Elaine looked up at Lonnie, her eyes wide with fear and revulsion. "Lonnie, can't you do something?" she asked, but Lonnie just took her hands in his, and she saw his jaw was set in that familiar stubborn way.

"No, honey, it's a fair fight. Tolbert will have ta finish it hisself."

Suddenly, the fight ended. While grappling on the ground for the knife, the Indian had been stabbed. Blood saturated the ground. A woman screamed hysterically. Elaine realized with surprise that the voice was her own.

Lonnie took her by the shoulders and shook her. "Elaine, git a'hold of yerrself. It's all over now." He pulled her shaking body close and held her while she sobbed.

When she got control of herself again, she looked up to see what the other Indians were going to do. To her surprise, they had vanished without a word. "Lonnie, I thought Indians took revenge when one of their own is killed. Where did they go? Is it over?"

"It's a long way from over," he answered grimly. "They'll come back, you can count on it, and there'll be the devil ta pay when they do."

Cold shivers of dread gripped Elaine as she could only try imagine a hordes of angry savages overrunning the wagon train, inflicting all type of dark, evil deeds on its occupants.

Two full days had gone by since the Indian had been stabbed, and Elaine had begun to breathe a sigh of relief. The sun shone brightly and the summer sky was the bluest of blue (about the color of Lonnie's eyes, she thought). Surely the men of the wagon train could ease their guard now. "If the Indians were going to attack, they would have shown themselves by now," she reasoned to herself.

However, Elaine didn't realize that the Indians did not reason with a white man's logic. True, the stabbing incident happened during a fair fight but they didn't see it that way. Michael had started the fight by offering them liquor then taking it back, so the fight that ensued was his fault in their opinion. A white man had killed their brother, and revenge would be sweet and sure.

Elaine caught her breath. What she saw turned her blood to ice. There, on the crest of the next hill, were Indians, scores of them, just standing there, waiting and watching. No longer were they ragtag beggars, but warriors, menacing and intimidating.

Buck came riding back to Lonnie and Elaine's wagon. "Hey, Lon! Saddle yer hoss and ride out with me ta parley with them red devils out there!" Without waiting for a response, he rode off to round up a couple of the other men whose judgment and temperament he trusted.

Elaine stood beside the wagon, hands to her chest, as Lonnie, Buck, and three or four others rode slowly toward the intimidating row of Indians who lined the horizon. The white flag that Buck carried flapped in the warm morning breeze. She saw with relief that a party of Indians were riding toward the white men. If they were willing to talk, perhaps Buck could persuade them to go back without a fight.

Silence engulfed the morning. The birds weren't even singing. An occasional whinny and the sound of horses hooves as the two groups of riders drew closer together were the only sounds she could hear.

From where she was standing, Elaine could see Buck and an Indian with a very large headdress exchange greetings. Then all riders dismounted and sat in a circle, legs crossed. She heard from Lonnie later what had been said.

"Greetings to you, old friend," said Two Horse, chief of the Ute nation. "Many moons have come and gone since you've visited our camp in the mountains."

"Greetings to you, Two Horse," responded Buck. "Fur tradin' ain't what it used ta be, I reckon."

They sat in silence, waiting for the Indians to make the next move. Lonnie felt the hair rise on the back of his neck at the realization that directly behind him were dozens of savages, who would just as soon take his scalp as look at him.

Two Horse remained silent and motionless for what seemed to be eons to Lonnie and the other settlers. Buck knew Two Horse was just biding his time, baiting the white men to see what they were made of. Buck looked proudly at the group of men he had brought with him. He knew their nerves were raw but to all outward appearances, they were calm and collected as a Sunday school class. Nobody spoke a word.

Finally, Two Horse motioned and one of his braves handed him a long pipe. Wordlessly, he filled it with a strong tobacco and lit it. Pointing it to all four directions, the Mother Earth and to Manitou in the sky, Two Horse puffed on the peace pipe and passed it to Buck, who went through the same ritual and passed it on. The ritual was repeated until the circle was completed and the pipe returned to Two Horse. At last, he spoke. "One of your men killed Swift Deer. Your man called Tolbert must die."

Expressionless, Buck considered what Two Horse said. "Two Horse speaks harsh words. Tolbert and Swift Deer fit a fair fight. Swift Deer was stabbed by accident. He fell on his own knife."

"Tolbert give my warriors firewater then tried to take it back. Swift Deer was fighting one who has no honor. Tolbert must die." Stone faced, Two Horse stared at Buck.

With a sweeping motion, he indicated the horizon still lined with warriors almost as far as you could see. With a sudden pointing motion, he continued, "Your people are few, they are weak. My people are warriors, yours are farmers." Two Horse turned his head to where he could look straight into Buck's eyes. "Send Tolbert to us and we will let your wagon train go in peace."

Two Horse stood in one motion. His braves stood with him. "We will meet here again as the sun rises tomorrow. If you do not bring Tolbert, all of you will die!"

Silently the men returned to the wagon train, the impending decision weighing heavily on them.

Buck called a meeting of the entire train. While everyone was gathering, Lonnie had explained to Elaine what was happening.

"Buck wouldn't just hand Michael over to them, would he?" she asked. "Just hand him over to be slaughtered like an animal?"

"Honey, I don't know what's gonna happen at this point. Buck knows his business and he'll do whatever he has ta do ta keep the wagon train safe." Seeing the look on her face he continued quickly, "Come on, the meeting is about ta start."

Buck stood in front of the solemn-faced crowd. They looked confused and very frightened. Noisily he spat a stream of tobacco juice and wiped his mouth with the back of his hand. Leaning on one arm against a wagon wheel, he got straight to the point. "Folks, we got ourselves a problem here and it ain't no little'un neither." Turning he faced the man who had caused it all. "Tolbert, them Injuns want your hide."

Michael Tolbert gasped and staggered as though he had been struck a blow. White-lipped, he said, "You can't hand me over to them. Please, I-I didn't do anything. That savage killed himself as we struggled over the knife. You all saw it! I didn't murder him! You all saw it!" he repeated desperately.

Buck raised his hand in a gesture for silence. "Tolbert, that don't make no difference ta Two Horse. Fact remains, you tolled them Injuns over to your wagon with a jug a'moonshine." Buck's bushy brows knitted together and his voice lashed out at the shaking man. "You *knew* better than that, Tolbert. I *told* ever' one'a you men a-fore we left Independence about keeping the whiskey away from the Injuns, and the grief that can come ta them that gives it to 'em." His eyes pierced Tolbert's. "Injun's seem ta go crazy with just a whiff'a that stuff."

Turning to the silent group of people in front of him he said, "Now, you folks have ta decide what ta do about Tolbert here. I reckon a vote is the only way ta settle it fair and square." "What we'll do," he continued, "is pass around a bucket. Sticks means we turn'im over ta Two Horse. Rocks means we stand and fight fer 'im."

One man spoke up from the back of the crowd. "Hand 'im over to the Injuns! He got his own self into this mess. Let 'im get hisself out of it!"

Buck held up his hands as several others joined in affirming that idea. "No, sir, we ain't gonna do it that-a way. We're gonna let ever' man vote so's no one can tell it later that he didn't have no say in it."

Jessie stood there, uncertain what to do. Buck nudged him and chided, "Hey, feller, jump in there and git you something to vote with!"

A harsh man's voice split the air. "You gonna let that darkie vote? Are you crazy? I shore wouldn't want one'a them decidin' life er death fer me!"

"On my train, mister, he's got jist as many rights as you do! He pulls his weight around here and I won't tolerate any more talk like that! Do I make myself clear?" Dead silence. "All right then, git to it!"

A big smile crossed Jessie's face. "Yassur! Ah bleeves Ah will do jist dat. Ah's a free man now!"

The people began murmuring softly to each other, milling around looking for sticks and stones to cast their ballots.

Buck took a bucket and went from man to man. Tolbert watched, almost hysterical, as the hands reached into the bucket, each ballot cast drawing him closer to his fate.

"Now folks, you stand and watch as these votes are counted. I don't want there to be any question about it," Buck said as the last ballot was cast. "There's 61 men to vote, 59 not countin' Tolbert and me. This has to be you folk's decision. I'll abide by it."

He turned and held the bucket out to Lonnie. "Come over here, boy, and count these votes."

Reluctantly Lonnie began pulling the ballots out of the bucket. "Twenty-five sticks and thirty-four rocks," he said as he removed the last ballot.

At those words, Michael's legs buckled and he began to weep uncontrollably. Elaine felt sick to her stomach. Some looked at him with contempt. Others just looked away uncomfortably.

Buck faced the people. "Well, you've voted ta stand and fight," he said matter-of-factly.

"Draw yore wagons in as tight as ya can. Wet down yore wagon covers in the mornin' a-fore daylight, because as soon as I go out and parley with Two Horse and tell'im he cain't have Tolbert, it won't be long till they'll be all over us."

Michael Tolbert appeared to his fellow travelers to be a weak man, full of fear. The fear engulfed him in a wave, but he was no fool. He suddenly realized one thing. No matter how the vote turned out, he was a dead man. The wagon train couldn't possibly withstand an onslaught by the formidable group he had seen on the horizon that morning. Under those circumstances, not only would he be killed, but all those innocent women and children would be killed or worse. With horror, he visualized the lovely Elaine lying dead in a pool of her own blood.

Elaine helped Lonnie secure the wagon as best they could. She could see Michael, drinking steadily, heavily. Anger and bitterness filled her as the reality set in that they would all likely die trying to save this worthless man.

She walked up to him and said scathingly, "Don't you think you've had enough of that stuff? After all, this whole situation is totally your fault. If you had been sober, we wouldn't all be in this mess to start with! Now, because of you, we're likely all going to be killed!"

Tolbert winced as though she had slapped him. "I fully realize my responsibility in this unfortunate situation, my dear," he replied formally. "However, never fear, things will be made right." After making a drunken attempt at a bow, he returned to his jug.

Elaine stomped back to the wagon. "That man is impossible, Lonnie! Here we are, all risking our lives to save him and he's just lying around getting drunk!"

Lonnie grunted. "That's the way his kind'a people are. Start a fire and walk off and leave it fer someone else ta put out!"

CHAPTER 13

———◉———

MOST EVENINGS AFTER SUPPER, YOU could hear strains of old familiar tunes from a fiddle or harmonica or guitars around the camp, accompanied by voices lifted in song and occasional bursts of laughter. Tonight was different. There was an eerie silence throughout the train. Families huddled together, talking in muted tones.

Buck drifted from wagon to wagon, giving reassurance and encouragement where he could. He walked up to where Lonnie and Elaine were sitting, holding hands and talking softly. "Evenin', folks!"

"Good evening, Buck," they replied in unison.

Lonnie nodded hospitably. "Set yourself down and rest a spell."

"Naw, I don't reckon I will, but thank ye kindly. Just thought I'd drop by and see if everything's all right."

"I guess we're as ready as we'll ever be," replied Lonnie. "The way Tolbert acted today almost made me wish we'd voted the other way." Lonnie poked the campfire violently and sparks flew wildly for a moment.

"I know what you mean, boy, but we didn't and we're bound to abide by the vote." Buck spat to one side. "Ma'am, if'n you got any pull with the 'Man Upstairs,' you might oughta use it ta' night." With a touch of his hat brim to Elaine, he walked away.

Elaine had been praying ever since the vote had been taken, but this time she took Lonnie's hand, and they bowed their heads and asked God to protect them in the conflict to come in the morning. "Dear Heavenly Father," Lonnie's soft, deep voice broke the silence in the camp. "You know, Lord, that none o' this is the fault of anyone here but Tolbert over there, but I beg fer your protection, not only fer us, but fer him as well. Help us to defeat this band of savages. Your will be done Lord. In Your Son Jesus's name I pray. Amen." Soft "amens" were heard around the camp.

Wild shrieks and bloodcurdling yells brought the wagon train to life just as the sun broke over the horizon. Thinking that the Indians hadn't waited to go through the formalities with Buck, the men grabbed their rifles and put their families in their designated places of safety. To their surprise, however, Two Horse and his men were not rushing the wagon train. Instead, they were milling around, about fifty yards out.

After full daylight, Buck, waving a white flag, rode out toward the excited Indians. As he drew closer, they drew back a little and Two Horse rode out to meet him. After the usual greetings he said, "White man surprised Two Horse. I did not think you would trade the dog Tolbert for the wagon train. Buck shows much wisdom in this decision."

Buck's jaw went slack in spite of himself. "What are you talkin' about?"

Two Horse motioned and Michael Tolbert appeared, being half dragged, half carried to the place where Two Horse and Buck sat astride their horses. "Tolbert, what happened?"

Tolbert looked up at Buck. "I figure dead is dead whether I go by myself or take the whole train with me. Go on back, Buck, and let them get it over with."

"Ya know I cain't help ya now, boy," said Buck with just a hint of a break in his voice.

"I know, it's all right. Tell Elaine to look in my wagon for a letter. Go on, please!" He looked at Buck with death in his eyes.

"God be with ya, boy," and with a heavy heart Buck went back to the wagon train to tell the others that Michael Tolbert had saved the day for them and that he was virtually committing suicide.

The wagon train began to move out. Buck's main concern was to get the women and children out of earshot of Tolbert's agonized shrieks, but a wall of warriors lined up in front of them. Running Wolf, Two Horse's right-hand man, told Buck matter-of-factly, "Two Horse say, wagons stay until dog Tolbert dies." Buck nodded in resignation.

Elaine would never forget that day as long as she lived. The Indians forced them to line up and watch as hour after horrible hour, they tortured Tolbert. She would hear his almost nonhuman screams in her mind for the rest of her life. At one point, she could smell burnt flesh and hair, and she prayed that God would take Michael and end his suffering. "Please, dear God, let it be over," she prayed.

About three o'clock that afternoon, Two Horse rode up to the place where the people from the wagon train were standing. Silently, he rode his horse at a slow pace looking them over as a military officer might inspect his troops. When he came to where Buck, Lonnie, and Elaine were standing, he pulled his horse to a stop and stared at Elaine. "Woman have hair like fire," he commented to Buck. As though in wonder, he reached down and touched her hair softly with the back of his hand. Lonnie stiffened as though to react but Buck took his elbow in a viselike grip, whispering, "Let it go, boy!"

Then suddenly, as if on a signal, the Indians rode off. They disappeared over the horizon as if they'd never been there.

From the mound on the ground they knew to be Tolbert, the screaming sounded hoarse and weaker now. Buck took the other men and rode out to him.

Elaine watched as Lonnie dismounted and after just a few seconds stepped behind the horses and became violently sick. A single gunshot split the air and then silence. She watched as the men buried Michael Tolbert where he lay.

Lonnie would never talk about what he saw that day, but she had learned from some of the other women that the Indians had seared Tolbert's eyes out with hot coals and had skinned the poor man alive. He had been scalped and his hands were missing. When the men had rode up, he had been writhing in agony and had begged Buck to have mercy on him and end his suffering. Buck's single bullet between the eyes had relived Tolbert's pain once and for all. What a cruel and violent country was this land west of the Mississippi! Would they never have a normal life again? The horror of it all was more than Elaine could comprehend.

As the wagon train prepared to roll out once more, Buck handed Elaine a folded paper. "Tolbert said to see ya got this," was all he said as he rode away. Elaine opened it up and read:

My Dearest Elaine,

Although I know I have no right to call you 'my dearest,' you will forever be that to me. I have loved you from the first day I saw you back in St. Louis. I know you and your family felt that I was not good enough for you, and isn't it funny, but I guess you were right after all! Be that as it may, I intend to turn myself over to those savages before dawn. I'm a dead man either way, and I can't bear to think that something I've done might bring harm to you, my dear girl. Please don't think too harshly of me.

Yours forever,
Michael

Tears coursed down Elaine's cheeks as she recalled his many attempts to win her favor and attention over the past year or so. The poor miserable man had really cared for her, and though she despised what he had become, she abhorred the end that had come to him.

The bit of paper dropped from her fingers as she climbed onto the wagon seat. They were rolling west again.

CHAPTER 14

LIFE WENT ON FOR THE pioneers after the horror of the Tolbert incident. Day after grueling day, mile after grinding mile, they went on, still focused on the new life waiting for them at the end of the trail. Occasionally they would catch a glimpse of Two Horse and his men riding parallel in the distance, but they never came close to the wagon train again.

Elaine had witnessed more tragedy since leaving Independence than she'd ever known in her entire young life, and she knew instinctively that even more would strike before they reached their destination. She didn't know how true her instinct would prove to be.

The loud, cruel man who called for Michael Tolbert to be handed over to the Indians without a vote drowned while trying to cross a swollen river. Two women died from sheer exhaustion, their delicate bodies unable to withstand the rigors of the trail. A young woman about her own age had died in childbirth. Both mother and baby had perished. Elaine didn't know them very well, but she felt very sad for the family. Then came that fateful day when tragedy struck with a force that would haunt her forever.

Thelma and Banjo Casey were good Irish Protestants. They were immigrating with their eight children from Kentucky where their families had settled back in the 1700s. The whole wagon train spoke about how well-behaved the Casey children were.

Thelma had become like a big sister to Elaine after her dress caught on fire that awful day. The two women, though not close in age, were kindred spirits, and the Rosses and the Caseys bonded and became as family as time went by.

Thelma watched with admiration as Elaine schooled her eight children and four or five others from families who lacked the education to teach themselves. She not only taught them the "three Rs" but also schooled them in the wisdom and salvation of the Lord, with Thelma's help.

One evening Elaine and Thelma were holding class as usual (evening because they were always on the move during the day). Their textbook was the Holy Bible. Thelma had hers, Elaine had one, and one or two of the other children each had one. So they shared and all made out quite nicely. Elaine loved listening to the lively discussions that erupted from time to time.

"But, Ma!" Thelma's oldest, Collin, said, "when Peter sliced off that varmint's ear, why didn't Jesus just call down the angels and have done with the lot of 'em? Why did He let Himself get carried off like that?"

To their surprise his eight-year-old sister, Colleen, spoke up. "I believe it was because God asked Jesus to do it that way. Is that right, Ma?"

"It certainly is, Lambie," replied Thelma, beaming at her daughter. Thelma had shared with Elaine recently that she sensed Colleen seemed to be getting close to a declaration of faith and thought it only a matter of time until she accepted Jesus as her Savior.

"Let's all say 'John 3:16' together and then I want someone to tell me what it means," said Elaine to the class.

The beautiful words rang out through the night and others around them stopped what they were doing for a moment to listen to the children's recitation. "For God so loved the world that He gave His only begotten Son, that whosoever believeth on Him should not perish, but have everlasting life."

Elaine looked around the class. "The scripture says, 'For God so loved the *world*.' Someone tell me who the 'world' is."

Once again, shyly, Colleen spoke up. "That's all of us, ain't it, ma'am? Every single person in the whole wide world?" She looked at her mother for support.

"Isn't," corrected Elaine. She then nodded to Thelma to go ahead and answer her daughter's question. "That's right, Lambie," Thelma replied, cupping her daughter's chin in a gesture of affection.

"And that's why Jesus scolded Peter when he cut off the man's ear. He knew God had sent Him to die for all people, even that man," said Colleen. Again showing wisdom beyond her eight years. "Ma, I think I understand now, and I want Jesus to be my Savior. I feel Him *here*!" The child's face glowed with a radiance sweet to look upon as she placed her little hands over her heart. Thelma took her by the hand and led her to a place where they could speak privately and pray together. Right there on the Oregon Trail, a small child reached out to the Lord, and He assured her a place in eternity.

The next day proved to be a rainy one, with a slight chill in the air as early morning found them moving again. The miserable travelers continued their trek west, most sloshing through muck and mud on foot. The Rosses and the Caseys were among the few who had room for some passengers on their wagons. Today the youngest of the eight Casey children, and Thelma, all crowded on board with Banjo to get some protection from the elements. The four oldest rode with Lonnie and Elaine, who were in line directly behind the Casey wagon.

Suddenly, everything went into slow motion for Elaine. Though it seemed to take forever, actually it was over in just a few tragic seconds. Elaine screamed, "Thelma! Stop! Stop! There's a sash hanging over the wheel!" but the noise of wagons and the children all talking and laughing at once drowned out her warning. Lonnie stopped the wagon as quickly as he could and bolted for the Caseys, but too late. The sash caught in the spokes of the wheel, and Elaine watched in horror as Colleen, sweet, smart little Colleen, was dragged from the wagon. Before Banjo could get the wagon stopped, she was crushed beneath the massive weight of the wheel.

A cry rang out, and Buck halted the train. He came riding back to see what the commotion was all about. He couldn't believe his eyes. Thelma was sitting on the ground holding her daughter, sobbing and asking, "My poor little Lambie! Why? Why?" over and over again. Poor Banjo stood dry-eyed and in shock. The rest of the children were screaming and crying, unable to comprehend the finality of what had just happened to their sister.

The men dug a grave, and every person on the train gathered to pay their respects to the little girl who had been like a ray of sunshine for so many of them.

Suddenly, the sun popped through the clouds. The drizzle stopped and the sky was so blue it made your heart ache. A few puffy white clouds were floating lazily along overhead. The sun bathed the faces of the mourners with warmth, as they gathered around the small grave. The respectful silence wrapped around the Casey family like a warm blanket. Occasionally, a cough or a sob could be heard from the grieving friends.

As they had no minister traveling with them, Thelma and Banjo asked Quentin Blakeford to say a few words, as they respected him highly. A godly man, full of encouragement, Quentin seemed to always know the right things to say in a crisis.

"We stand here today to bury one of the sweetest little girls that God ever made. Colleen had a way about her that just warmed a body's heart!"

Many of the mourners nodded and smiled at the memories his words brought up. "Now, we can't even begin to make sense of this tragedy. All we can do is to trust God to give comfort that only He can at a time like this. Thelma told me that Colleen had only just yesterday trusted the Lord as her Savior, and I know there's not a doubt in anyone's mind where this sweet child is right this minute!" He turned to the grieving brothers and sisters. "Children, don't try to think about Colleen and the accident. Instead, just know this. Right now, up in heaven, Jesus Himself is holding her close, rocking her and loving her the way only He can."

There was a visible straightening of Thelma's back as she listened to Mr. Blakeford's comforting words. Yes, she *could* take comfort in knowing that Colleen was with Jesus. She believed that with all her heart and in her mind's eye she could visualize Christ holding her baby girl. What a bittersweet picture that was to the grieving mother, and oh, how she would miss her little Lambie.

Mr. Blakeford finished up his brief message. "Please join me in reciting the Twenty-third Psalm. 'The Lord is my Shepherd, I shall not want,'" his deep voice recited the familiar passage and very softly, those who knew it joined in.

When the service was over, the people slowly filed by the Caseys, hugging them, crying with them, until at last, only the family remained. Suddenly, the air was filled with the children's voices saying, "For God so loved the world that He gave His only begotten Son …" As John 3:16 filled the air, the women began to prepare the noon meal. They would resume their travel as soon as it was done. Not even death could slow them. They were racing against the elements. They must cross the Great Divide before winter set in.

CHAPTER 15

ELAINE HAD NO IDEA THAT mountains could be as tall as the majestic Rockies proved to be. They kept climbing and climbing, going higher and higher, the thin air and steep terrain making it very difficult to progress with any speed. In early September, they crested the Great Divide, and as they did, large, beautiful, well-defined flakes of snow began to fall. The pioneers' prayers were answered, however, as the heavy snow waited until they were safely down the other side. Their long, arduous journey was drawing to a close.

Three weeks later, it appeared! A green valley spread before them, lush and fragrant as far as the eye could see. Two mountain ranges, just visible on the far horizons, framed the valley. One particular mountain range caught Elaine's eye as she stared wide-eyed at the most beautiful place she had ever seen. "Lonnie, look at those mountains over there! It almost looks like a hand with the forefinger pointing upward. Isn't that the strangest thing?"

Lonnie followed her gaze. "That's what they call 'the Hand of God,' honey." That's where we're going to settle. Right over there below that old mountain," Lonnie told her.

The morning dawned cool as pink fingers of light filtered through the sparse clouds that floated teasingly around the mountain tops. Lonnie and Elaine drank in their first view of the green valley. They stared at it in silence, the beauty of it so intense that neither of them could speak. They agreed with no doubt about it. They were home. The Caseys and several other families also chose to make the beautiful valley their home as well.

The settlers had to work quickly for winter would soon be upon them. First priority, shelter for everyone. They worked together to help each other build cabins on the homesteads that they had staked out. First, for the families with children, such as Thelma and Banjo, then the older folks, and then the young people, such as Lonnie and Elaine.

All the cabins were pretty much the same, one large room with a lean-to on the back. Lonnie added a tiny front porch for Elaine so they could sit together as they rested after a long day. There was no time to plant a garden or clear fields for crops, so the women gathered up all the wild plants they could to help sustain their families through the long, cold Oregon winter. Wild greens such as poke, dock, sheep sorrel, and lamb's quarter were plentiful, and the ladies canned as much as they could. Wild onions and berries of all kinds were picked and dried or canned for later use.

The men hunted game: deer, quail, rabbits, squirrel, and wild turkey. They cooked and canned the meat, or smoked or dried it into jerky. With this addition to their diet, the settlers could survive until spring.

CHAPTER 16

Elaine thought she had seen deep snow back in St. Louis, but it paled in comparison to what they experienced that first winter in Oregon. It drifted so high it covered their little cabin. Lonnie peeked out into the lean-to. "It's still intact," he told Elaine. "Let's see if we can dig our way up so we can get to the roof and uncover our chimney." They carefully tunneled up through the deep snow until they were able to just step right out onto the roof! Quickly they cleared off the chimney and the area around it.

Elaine scooped up a large bowlful of snow, added sugar and vanilla, and made snow ice cream. It tasted wonderful! "You know what this reminds me of, dearest?" she asked.

"What's that?" Lonnie replied, his mouth full of ice cream.

"Do you remember the ball when we first met, and all the food there?"

Lonnie nodded and smiled. "I sure do! Me and my friends had never in our lives seen nuthin' like that!" His smile turned into a chuckle. "We didn't get ta stay very long, as I recollect!" They laughed at the memory of that first meeting.

"I'll be so glad when spring comes. I have letters written to Mama and Papa and all my friends. I can't wait to hear back from them." Elaine's eyes sparkled as she thought of her family and friends back home.

Lonnie cupped her face in his hands. "Mrs. Ross, yore the prettiest girl I've ever known." He kissed the tip of her nose. "Are ya sorry for all ya give up ta come with me?" He spoke lightly, but Elaine could tell he was serious.

"Well, Mr. Ross, I'll tell you. I most certainly am *not* sorry. I'd do it all over again. Every bit of it! The dust, the horrible food, death, Indians, sickness, nothing could ever make me sorry I married you!"

Lonnie took her into his arms and kissed her lovingly. "Good!" he said teasingly. "I'd hate ta have ta train a new woman!" Elaine smacked him on the shoulder and chased him around the cabin. They spent the rest of the snowy day in each other's arms, reinforcing their love for one another.

Spring finally arrived! The snow melted, and the signs of new life were everywhere! That first winter had been hard, but after all they'd been through on the trail, they felt they could conquer anything. They had survived, and they were ready to start their new life in their new home in this magnificent place!

The to-do list, though long, was undaunting to the young pioneers. Cut logs for a fence. Clear stumps and make a field for their crops. Wheat, corn, and oats were the staple crops. Then a garden plot must be cleared. Without a garden they would starve to death. There was no Farmer's Market like back home. They had brought all kinds of vegetable seeds from home, along with potato and onion sets. It was backbreaking work but Lonnie and Elaine toiled side by side and gradually, their little home below the mountain started to take shape.

Fatigue overtook Elaine after working in the vegetable garden all day. She came into the cabin and collapsed into the rocking chair. They had brought the rocker at Nanny's insistence. Nanny had rocked her in it as a baby and all the way up to the point that she was embarrassed to let her. Thoughts of Nanny brought tears of homesickness to her eyes.

Elaine did miss her family and friends very much, and sometimes she allowed herself to remember the pampered life she led back in St. Louis. She felt as though she was thinking of someone else, like pictures in a book! Tenderly, she opened a small cedar chest her mother had given to her the day she left. She had told her daughter that she wasn't to open it until she felt very homesick. She believed today would qualify! Carefully she opened the catch and lifted the lid. To her delight, music filled the room. A music box! How wonderful! She listened to the entire tune, delighted with her surprise. Carefully, she unwrapped a small packet. Inside lay a note from her mother.

> Daughter, if you are reading this you must be feeling pretty homesick today. Inside this packet are flower seeds from the flowers in our garden here at home. Plant them, darling, and remember when they bloom they are kisses from your Papa and me. Save the other things in the box for another blue day, for you are sure to have more than one. We all do. You and your Lonnie are constantly in our prayers. Goodbye, my darling. Remember, we love you.
>
> Signed, Mama

At that point, Elaine allowed herself a good cry, then scolded herself and took the wonderful present out to show to Lonnie.

CHAPTER 17

They had been in their new home for two years already, but it really didn't seem that long to the newlyweds. Happily for them, their friends, the Casey family, had decided to settle nearby. In fact, most of the people on the wagon train had chosen to settle at some point all up and down the beautiful valley under the watchful care of the Hand of God.

Lonnie and Buck had become very close during the five months it took to make the trip from Independence, Missouri, to the Oregon Territory. Lonnie and Elaine had used all their persuasive powers and had finally convinced their crusty old friend to give up his wandering ways.

Buck had led the wagon train on to the end of the trail, but once his commitment had been met, he returned to the valley. There he built himself a small cabin, just a couple of miles from them. They shared the work and joy and hardship, and were like family to each other.

Fortunately for Elaine, the threatening sky withheld its deluge until she was safely back into the cabin. She set the two heavy buckets of water on the table, and taking the pistol out of her apron pocket, she slid it under the featherbed in the corner. The one room served as kitchen, living room, bedroom, and dining room. As she hung her "everyday" bonnet on a peg, she laughed out loud at the thought of the fainting spell her mother would have if she could see how her daughter was living!

Nanny would have been scandalized at the sight of her delicate "L'il Missy" cooking, ironing, scrubbing clothes on a washboard down at the creek and doing all the things she had to do for them to survive in the wilderness.

With the coming of autumn came about a month of solitude for Elaine. Lonnie and Buck went trapping for furs to trade for supplies that they would need to get them through the winter. She hated being separated from her husband, but she really didn't mind being alone. Being surrounded with such beauty and tranquility gave her a feeling of real communion with God. The mountains reminded her of His majesty. The beauty of the valley around her reminded her of His goodness and mercy. The river that never ran dry reminded her that God is eternal. She often sat on her little front porch and pondered those things. With the shape of the mountain nearby, she truly felt she was in God's hand.

In her mind's eye, she could see Lonnie. She remembered the way he looked the day he and Buck had set off for the mountain, straddling their enormous old mare, Nancy, and leading a pack mule. His blue eyes were snapping with excitement. His broad shoulders strained at the cloth of his shirt. Those big, gentle hands that had, only moments before, held her face tenderly as he kissed her goodbye were now handling the lines controlling the rebellious mule as though it were nothing at all.

Unruly blond hair stuck out from under that old straw hat that she had thrown away a half dozen times, but Lonnie would always retrieve it from the rubbish pile. Finally, Elaine had conceded defeat and they had a good laugh over it. She would worry about her rugged, pioneer husband until she saw him ride back into the yard again, safe and sound. However, it helped so much to know that Buck was going with him.

The pampered girl that Lonnie Ross had married existed no more. Elaine smiled ruefully at the reflection in a small mirror over the washstand. Gone the flawless, creamy complexion that Nanny had guarded so faithfully. If she caught her outside without a sunbonnet on, oh, dear Gussie! Did she ever scold! "You gits yore bonnet on right now, Li'l Missy! Dem freckles gwine pop out on you lak popcorn and dat's a fac'!" Elaine giggled again at the thought of dear old Nanny's scoldings. "Dem freckles shorely *did* pop lak popcorn, Nanny, an' dat's a fac'!" Elaine mimicked. She truly hated those freckles, and Lonnie loved to tease her about them. She had come to accept the fact that her beautiful white skin was a thing of the past. Living in the frontier required one to be outdoors a lot. Almost everything they did was out-of-doors, field work, gardening, or doing their wash down at the creek, but she loved it! The hard work, though definitely challenging, gave her a sense of accomplishment and self-worth that surpassed any she'd ever known.

A magnificent clap of thunder startled Elaine and through the window she watched as a brilliant bolt of lightning flashed, leaving as quickly as it had come, a negative of itself remaining across the sky. She was somewhat frightened of the thunderstorms out here. They came up so quickly, out of nowhere it seemed, and were more intense than any she had seen between here and St. Louis. However, they also reminded her of God, and how powerful He is.

Trying to get her mind off the storm, she poked at the coals in the cooking hearth and set about getting a nice blaze going. She hung the tea kettle on the hook and soon it began its hissing symphony. Elaine had adjusted well to cooking over the open hearth, for she had learned much from the other ladies on the wagon train. She knew Lonnie longed for the day when he could buy her a nice new cookstove, with a water reservoir and a warming closet and an oven big enough to roast the biggest turkey he could find! She took a loaf of fresh bread from the breadbox and sliced off a generous portion for herself. She spread it thickly with a layer of sweet creamy butter that she had churned just that morning from old Daisy's rich milk. She poured a cup of hot tea and sat down to her simple feast at the rough-hewn table Lonnie had made for her with his own two hands.

"I never thought it would be possible for me to love any man the way I love you, Lonnie Albert Ross," she said softly. Perhaps, someday, if God answered her prayers, she could give Lonnie a son. "Lonnie Albert Ross, Jr.," she mused with a smile, "and won't he be something!"

Elaine bowed her head and gave thanks for her food, then attacked it with gusto. She finished her bread and butter, then took her hot tea and went out on the front porch. Each evening she and Lonnie loved to sit out there and take in the panoramic sunsets over the unusual mountain formation she had come to know as the Hand of God.

Their little front porch was special to Elaine. Most of their neighbors' cabins didn't have a porch, but Lonnie had built a tiny one for the two of them to sit on. It was their special place where they could drink in the beauty of the statuesque oaks, the spiraling pines and the snowcapped mountains. Three seasons out of the year the wild flowers were incredible—blues, reds, golds, yellows, and whites made the view so breathtaking that Elaine always got a lump in her throat each time she saw it.

As the sun disappeared slowly behind the mountain and the rain clouds slowly moved out of the valley, the sky displayed pink and gray splashes. Sleepy birds chirped to each other as they settled in for the night. Off in the distance, the whippoorwills were just waking up, their cries echoing from one end of the valley to the other.

Elaine sat as long as she could, spellbound by the magnificence of the world around her, but she was so tired that her head began to nod. She stood up and "stretched a mile" as Nanny used to say, and went back inside her little home.

CHAPTER 18

———◉———

ELAINE HAD NEVER BEEN A religious sort of girl back home in St. Louis. She had always felt God's love in her life because of Nanny's influence, but had never really made Him a real part of her life. Her mother, being French, grew up Catholic, but she hadn't really practiced her faith. Elaine's father hadn't been particularly religious until his talk with Nanny just before they started for Oregon, but he had found the contacts he could make at the large Presbyterian Church to be very beneficial to his business. So the Dentons had attended there off and on for as long as she could remember. Elaine remembered that church to be very formal. She recalled fondly when her parents would occasionally allow her to attend the Baptist church with Nanny. How wonderful those services had been! Heartfelt singing, everyone praising Jesus with their hands in the air, and all the "Amens and Hallelujahs" were very exciting to her. Sometimes they even shouted and danced in the aisle. She didn't tell Mama about that part. In that small black church, Elaine accepted Jesus as her Savior at age eleven.

The hardships and the struggles as they had traveled west had caused Elaine's faith to grow, and she found that she leaned on God to give her strength and courage she didn't have on her own. After reaching their new home, she continued to lean on Him, reading her Bible and praying faithfully every day. She felt very close to Him now and relied on her faith to sustain her when she felt her strength ebb.

Most of the time, day's end found her to be so tired she could barely keep her eyes open, but she never failed to read at least a verse or two from the well-worn Bible she kept on the mantle. This evening she made no exception. She turned to the Psalms, chapter 121. "I will lift up mine eyes to the hills, from whence cometh my help," she read. She paused and thought, "From whence cometh my husband, too, very soon I hope!" She smiled at her own wit, blew out the lamp, and drifted off to sleep.

Lonnie felt good! He had a nice tidy little stack of pelts on his mule—enough to take Elaine in to the Windy Creek settlement and let her buy a pretty piece of material for a new dress! He grinned as he imagined her excitement when he revealed the surprise. His grin faded as his thoughts continued. "Poor little gal," he thought to himself, "you ain't had a new dress since we come out here but ya never complain."

The furs Lonnie collected by trapping beaver each fall allowed him to lay in enough supplies to last until the next spring. Many of the homesteaders existed this way—farming in the spring, summer and early fall and trapping in the late fall and sometimes early spring. Even with all this, they still led a hand-to-mouth existence.

From his lofty vantage point, Lonnie watched as the thunderheads rolled out over the valley below. Lonnie's pulse quickened as he thought how he would be with his sweet little wife again in just a few hours. He wished he were there now, for he knew she would be frightened of the storm.

As he followed his old friend down the twisting trail, Lonnie felt a rush of affection. He didn't know very much about Buck. He never spoke of his past and Lonnie never pried. He knew that he was about fifty-something years old and had come from somewhere in Illinois.

"You know, boy, sometimes I wisht I'd-a took up with one-a them Injun gals back in my younger days." He punctuated his sentence with a stream of tobacco juice. "Them long winter nights gits mighty lonely sometimes."

"Well, now, from the way Banjo Casey was tellin' it to me, the Widow Burton over at the settlement has kind-a took a shine to ya," bantered Lonnie.

This time the stream of spittle came with a vengeance. "Don't I know that? Ever' time I go over there she has ta latch on-ta me like a stick-tight! She made me go ta her house and eat sweet-tater pie the last time I seen her. I don't even *like* sweet-tater pie!" Again the tobacco juice shot forth. "She jist flits around me like a bee!"

Lonnie's laughter echoed across the canyon.

The cabin creaked companionably as the wind sighed through the pines outside. Elaine was having a wonderful dream in which she and Lonnie were laughing together over some private joke as they worked side by side, when she awoke with the terrifying awareness that she was not alone in the cabin. She lay rigid with fear as a shadow moved stealthily about in the pale moonlit room. Slowly, not even breathing, she slid her hand under the featherbed where she lay until it came in contact with cold steel.

Her heart pounded in her ears as she slid the gun free and cocked it, very slowly. "Whoever you are, I can see your shadow as plain as day. Don't move until I get the lamp lit or I'll shoot you right where you stand!" Her voice came out calm and even, not showing at all the fear she was feeling.

The shadow froze in the moonlight. At that moment, the lamp lit and a chagrined Lonnie stood looking at a very white-faced Elaine. She threw the gun down onto the bed and ran over to him. He lifted her off the floor for a very long passionate kiss.

"Lonnie Albert Ross! I almost shot you! What do you mean sneaking up on a body that way? You, of all people, should have known better—" He kissed her again. "But I could have shot you" was smothered by another kiss. He kissed her again and again, each time she tried to scold. His blue eyes twinkled wickedly. "There now, ain't that better?" he teased, as she finally gave up.

She hugged him tight then whacked him playfully on the shoulder and set about preparing breakfast as the first faint lines of dawn had begun to creep into the sky.

CHAPTER 19

As spring turned into summer, it became obvious to Elaine that one of her prayers had been answered. She felt certain that she was pregnant! Of course, this would just be the first in the long line of fine healthy children that she and Lonnie planned to have. Large families were almost a necessity for the homesteaders. A staggering workload burdened the pioneer families as they carved their homes out of the Oregon wilderness. The more children they had, the more helping hands there were.

Elaine waited patiently for the perfect moment to tell Lonnie the good news, but the time just never seemed right. He was busy from dawn till dusk, and most evenings it seemed she watched the sunset alone to the accompaniment of Lonnie's exhausted snoring. He had seemed preoccupied since he'd returned from trapping last fall, but when she asked him he'd just make a joke and deny anything was bothering him. She had noticed an estrangement between Lonnie and their old friend Buck. Something had happened while they were out trapping. Neither of them would talk about it, but when Buck dropped by, Lonnie would disappear. She desperately wanted to help but didn't have a clue where to start.

Well, she couldn't let that bother her right now. She made up her mind that today would be the day Lonnie would find out he was going to be a father! She did up the breakfast dishes and straightened up the cabin, then she went to find Lonnie. She cornered him in the cow lot.

"Lonnie Ross, will you stand still for one minute, please? I've been trying to tell you something for weeks!"

"What is it, honey?" he asked absentmindedly, forking more hay in to old Daisy.

"Do you think you could get a cradle made by January?" she asked softly.

Abstractedly he said, "Oh, sure, honey, I'll get started on it—uh, *what did you say?*"

With shining eyes, Elaine made a rocking motion with her arms. The amazed father-to-be suddenly sat down on the edge of the cow tank, as though his legs had just given way. As he continued to stare speechless at Elaine, he lost his balance and fell in, feet straight up! He came up sputtering and grinning like a Cheshire cat! He hopped out of the tank, grabbed Elaine and gave her a soggy hug.

All that day he'd say, "A baby, well, what do you know about that!" Needless to say, a cradle was indeed begun right away, and into it were built many loving hopes and dreams for the new member of the Ross household!

Elaine had a very unremarkable pregnancy, and she felt almost apologetic when she wrote to her mother that she had never had even one session with morning sickness. (She didn't tell her that Buck patted her on the back and said she was "as tough as a Ute squaw!" Mama would not see the humor in that remark.)

The months sped by and before they knew it, it was time for the baby to come. Elaine awoke early one morning slightly more uncomfortable than usual. She had given up looking for a comfortable position to sit, stand or lie in for about the last two months!

"Lonnie, you'd better ride over and get Thelma. I think it's time."

Elaine had to laugh at her poor, nervous husband. He was so shook up she had to help him button his shirt! His big fingers were shaking so badly that he couldn't get them to work for him.

Taking his rifle, Lonnie stepped outside and fired three shots in the air. One, then wait, then quickly, two more. "Honey, I think I'll be all right until you and Thelma get back. There's really no need to bother Buck. My twinges may not be the real thing anyway."

Lonnie turned to her and tenderly chucked her under the chin. "Hey, woman," he said softly, "yore the most precious thing in my life and yore carryin' my child. I'm not gonna go off fer hours and leave you alone and in labor. Now, you go back inside and git off yore feet. The old man'll be here directly." He hurried out to the corral to saddle Nancy. As he rode out for the Casey place he could see Buck riding at breakneck speed coming in from the other way. Lonnie lifted his hand and Buck waved back.

Thinking of all the work that needed to be done, and feeling rather like a child playing hooky, Elaine went back inside and lay down on the bed. She didn't want to do anything to bring her labor on any faster. She sure didn't want Buck to have to act as midwife!

Pretty soon the familiar pounding came at the door, and Buck called out, "Is anybody ta home?"

"Come on in, Buck, the door's open!"

The old mountain man, turned wagon master, turned farmer, stepped inside, his floppy old hat in his hands. "Mornin', gal!" he said uncomfortably. Before he shut the door he stuck his head out and spat. "You all right?"

"Just a little uncomfortable right now. Lonnie went over to the Casey's to get Thelma. I think I'll be fine, Buck, really. There's no need for you to have to stay here," said Elaine bravely.

"Now, you jist hold on a minute, Gal! I'm a-gonna stay here with ya till he gits back and there's no need ta discuss it no more," said Buck, his jaw set.

"Thank you, Buck, I really appreciate it, you know." Elaine patted his hand.

Embarrassed, Buck said, "You had yore breakfast?"

"I really couldn't eat a thing, thank you anyway," said Elaine.

He began stoking up the fire and rummaging around in the larder. "Wal, I'll jist fix me a bite if ya don't mind." Elaine told him he was welcome to anything he could find.

As he placed sizzling pieces of salt pork into the frying pan, Elaine began to feel queasy. Well, for heaven's sake! Morning sickness on the very last day! The nausea became worse and worse. She buried her head into the pillow, but she just couldn't escape the smell. Suddenly she jumped out of bed and dashed out of the cabin.

CHAPTER 20

A FTER HER HEAD CLEARED, SHE wiped her sweaty brow with her hanky. She felt the chill of the January wind through her flannel night gown. Shivering, she started back around the house toward the door, when two Indians materialized as if out of nowhere! She looked up in fear and shock at the painted faces. *Two Horse*, she thought, and fainted for the first time in her life.

When Elaine came to, she was lying in her own bed and her labor was becoming intense. Buck was sitting beside her, rubbing her wrists and wiping her face with a cool cloth. "Elaine," he was saying, using her name for the first time since she'd known him. "Elaine, come on, honey, wake up. You gotta a big job ta do, gal." Worry was etched in every line in his face.

"Buck, the Indians—what-what happened?" she asked weakly.

"Them savages won't be botherin' nobody else, I reckon," Buck replied grimly. "I put 'em ta goin' with my trusty pistol."

"Are you all right?" she asked with sudden fear.

"Yeah, they never teched me!" he said, grinning proudly. The big grin faded quickly, however, as Elaine's face contorted in pain as her body was racked with another contraction.

"Is Lonnie back yet?" she asked when she could speak.

"No'm, he's not back yet, but should be 'bout any time now."

Lonnie pushed Nancy as fast as she would go. Thelma Casey had earned the reputation as an excellent midwife, and he needed to get her back to the cabin as soon as possible. "I'm gonna be a Pa!" The thought made him remember the talk he and Buck had on the mountain last fall.

"When you was a young fella, did ya ever think about marriage, Buck?" Lonnie asked, hesitantly, for he'd never asked Buck anything so personal about his past before.

Buck got a sad faraway look in his eyes. "Done more'n thought about it, truth be told, I reckon. I'm ashamed ta tell ya this, Lon, but since ya asked I guess I will." Lonnie looked at his old friend in mild surprise. He had never dreamed Buck had ever been anything other than a loner, living pretty much to himself.

"Go on," Lonnie coaxed.

"Back in '28 I married the purtiest lil' gal you ever laid eyes on. We got us a little farm just east of the Mississip', near St. Looey." Lonnie's eyes were now riveted on Buck. "But like I says, Lon, I'm ashamed ta say, the wanderlust got a-hold a'me, and about a year and a half later, I jist up and took off." Buck was holding his head in his hands by now. "I figured my woman would go back ta her people and find somebody who was worthy of her."

Lonnie's eyes never left Buck's face. "I've never heard yore real name in all the years I've known ya, Buck. What is it?" he asked stiffly.

"Well, funny enough, my last name's Ross, same as yourn. Never figured it made no difference. Last names jist git in the way sometimes."

Lonnie's face had locked into a hard, rigid look. "What's your whole name, Buck? Is it John Albert Ross, by any chance?"

"Why, yes, it is, but how in tarnation—?" Buck started to say.

"And yore wife's name. You know, the one ya ran off and left on a farm east of St. Louis?"

"Elizabeth," Buck said softly.

"And her maiden name was Holmes, I reckon," Lonnie said, his voice harsh.

"Why, that's exactly it, but how in tarnation do ya know that?" Buck asked incredulously.

Lonnie stood up and looked down at the man seated on the ground below him. The man he had dreamed about and looked for in the face of every other man he'd ever met. The man he'd dreamed would come back to him and Ma and they'd all live happily ever after, just like in the storybooks. "I know because after you left, I was born. I'm yore son!" Lonnie practically spat those words as he mounted up and rode off toward the green valley and Elaine.

CHAPTER 21

As Lonnie rode into the valley where the Caseys lived, the similarity of their places struck him. The same small cabin (theirs did not have a porch; however, it did have two rooms because of size of the family), the same lean-to barn, the same small cow lot and corral, the same huge garden in the back and "acres and acres of stumps ta clear"! Lonnie thought ruefully.

By the time he reached the cabin, the whole Casey clan ran out to meet him. They seldom had company and they considered it a grand occasion when someone did stop by! Banjo Casey, nicknamed for the instrument he loved to play, smiled a smile that practically encompassed his round face. His plump, jolly wife, Thelma, standing a head taller than Banjo, stood smoothing her apron and occasionally cuffing one of their seven children for some mischief or other. The children stood as if by a predesigned plan in perfect stair-step formation. Each child's name began with a *C*, but for the life of him, Lonnie never could remember them all.

Lonnie pulled up and dismounted, tipping his hat to Mrs. Casey. "Yes, sir! Yes, sir! climb down there, Lonnie! By cracky, I don't recollect the last time we laid eyes on ya, boy!" cried Banjo, clapping him on the back.

Thelma, always the good hostess, said cordially, "Are ya hungry, Lonnie? We were just gettin' ready to sit down ta breakfast if ya care ta come in."

Nervously shuffling from one foot to the other Lonnie said, "Thank ya, kindly, ma'am, but I came ta see if you could come ta our place and help Elaine." Looking obliquely at the children, Lonnie floundered trying to find a tactful way to tell Thelma that Elaine's labor had started.

"Land sakes, Boy, don't worry about these kids! When you've got seven, they all pretty well know where babies come from!" laughed Thelma good-naturedly. The children all giggled and punched each other knowingly.

"I'll git my bonnet and my bag and I'll be ready ta go." Giving instructions to her family as she busied around getting her things together, she handed Lonnie a large piece of buttered cornbread. By this time, Banjo had their old mule, Eustis, saddled, and with much pushing and shoving from her husband, she climbed aboard. The old mule waited patiently while she got her plump self settled.

As they rode off together, Lonnie tried to curb his impatience at the slow plodding pace that old Eustis set, while Thelma blew kisses to her waving children until they were out of sight.

"I can't tell ya how much I appreciate you comin' ta help us out like this," said Lonnie gratefully.

"Land sakes, Lonnie! And what are friends for I always say, if we can't help one another?" she replied in her kind, blunt way.

They rode along in silence, Thelma's plump body jiggling with every step the old mule took. The sun was high in the late winter sky, and it was almost warm, even if it was January. She loosened the wool scarf she'd wrapped around her neck.

They reached an icy stream and stepped down to stretch their legs while they watered their mounts. "Well, it won't be long till we'll be there," commented Lonnie. "I hated ta go off and leave her by herself, but I signaled for Buck ta come up ta the house ta be with her while I was gone." His blue eyes were clouded with worry as he heaved Thelma unceremoniously back up onto her mule.

She leaned over and patted his shoulder. "Don't you worry, son. Your little wife will do just fine." She laughed infectiously. "Women just naturally have a way of doing these things without help from anyone, especially a man!" She chuckled at her own joke.

Lonnie smiled back, reassured temporarily, but his reassurance was short-lived. They had gone but a short distance when they heard shots. There it went again, definitely over by the cabin! Lonnie's heart leapt to his throat! Elaine! Something was bad wrong. Lonnie turned white as a sheet. He gouged Nancy mercilessly until she indignantly trotted as quickly as she could toward home.

Thelma followed more slowly behind. When she got to the house, grunting and groaning, she dismounted and tied old Eustis up next to Nancy at the hitching rail. She hurried inside. Lonnie cradled Elaine in his arms as she lay on the bed. "Are ya sure yore okay, honey?" he asked her as Thelma walked in.

"Yes, I'm okay, except for the labor pains." She groaned as another contraction grabbed her.

Quickly Thelma assessed the situation. "You, Buck, git some water to boilin'. Lonnie, we're gonna need lotsa towels and sheets. And somethin' ta wrap the baby in when he comes!" Barking orders like a drill sergeant, Thelma set about to help introduce the newest member of the Ross household into the world.

After the men got everything that Thelma had asked for, she shooed them out. "You'll just be in the way. Now git on outside. I'll call ya when the little one arrives," she said with a smile.

Lonnie and Buck sat on the little front porch, wincing with sympathy each time Elaine cried out in pain. "Tell me agin, Buck, what happened this mornin'?" said Lonnie.

"Well, sir, I wuz startin' ta fry me up a pan'a fatback and she took sick and ran outside. She warn't wearin' nothin' but her little nightgown so I grabs me up a blanket ta wrap her up in, but when I steps outside, there wuz two Utes bendin' over her. I thought she wuz dead, Lon, I swear it plum scared me ta death! I dropped that blanket and pulled my gun. They lit out fer cover, but I nailed 'em a-fore they got very fur." Buck wiped his brow with his bandana. "'Bout that time, she groaned and moved and glory be! She wuz fine! She'd jist fainted when she seen them Injuns. I got her back inta the house and come outside here and took a look-see all around. I reckon them two wuz out on their own. I never seen no sign of any more of 'em. She said it was Two Horse and one o' his braves, but I b'lieve she musta been mistaken. I jist don't figure as how he'd come all this way over here. Anyways, whoever they be, we need ta bury 'em a-fore their friends come a-lookin'."

The two men walked silently to the spot where Buck had shot the two braves. "Well, I be dogged!" exclaimed Buck. "They wuz a' layin' right there but they shore ain't now! I guess my aim wasn't as true as I thought it wuz." They both knew the possible consequences of Buck's missed shot, but right now they had more important things to think about.

They walked back to the house and sat down on the porch. They were silent for a long time, listening to the sounds coming from the house as Elaine's contractions became harder and harder. Lonnie clenched his fists in sympathy. Finally he spoke. "I want ta thank ya, Buck, fer savin' ma wife," he said softly, so softly Buck barely caught his words.

"No need ta thank me, Lon. I love that little gal like she wuz my own."

Lonnie smiled and nodded then took a deep breath. "Buck, ever since me and you was up on the mountain last fall, I know I've been purty ugly to ya."

Buck interrupted. "Now, Lon, that's okay," he started to say, but Lonnie cut him off.

"No, hear me out. I've hated you ever' since I was a kid, fer goin' off and leavin' Ma like that—fer not bein' there when I was born ta help out and such. I hated you fer the hard times me and Ma had, just tryin' ta git enough ta eat."

Unnoticed by either of them, tears began coursing down Buck's cheeks.

Lonnie went on. "I hated ya, Buck, but I loved ya too. I know that sounds crazy and I cain't rightly explain it, but I looked at ever' man I saw, wonderin', 'Is that my Pa?' I wondered whatcha looked like, what yore voice sounded like when ya spoke." Tears were now flowing down Lonnie's cheeks as well.

"I used to go fishin' and pretend you was sittin' there beside me. I'd talk to ya, tellin' ya my hopes and dreams about goin' west someday." He cleared his throat and wiped his eyes. "Then that day I found out who ya was, all that hate and disappointment jist about knocked me over. I couldn't take it all in. I had known ya fer a long time as a man, a good man, one that I trusted and called friend. I was so confused I jist needed time ta get things sorted out."

Buck placed his hand on his son's shoulder. "Son," Buck said, and Lonnie's heart beat faster at the sound of the word, "I wantcha ta know that I ain't got no excuse ta offer. I wuz young and had the 'wanderlusts' so bad I jist couldn't stand it. But this I promise ya, if I had knowed that yore Ma wuz carryin' you, I 'da never left." Buck wiped his eyes again. "Do ya believe me, son, and kin ya ever fergive me?" Emotion filled his voice.

Lonnie looked at his father, so full of remorse and sorrow for the past. Could he forgive him? "Yes, Pa," he said, using a term he'd dreamed of his whole life. "I fergive ya and I welcome ya into our lives. I wantcha ta be Pa and Grandpa. We're family." The two stood and as Thelma opened the door she saw father and son embrace for the first time in their lives.

She politely cleared her throat and said, "Lonnie?"

Both men turned toward her, wiping their eyes and Buck blowing his nose loudly into his bandana. "Yes, ma'am?" they both answered at the same time.

"Come inside and meet your daughter," Thelma said, smiling.

"Did you say 'daughter'?" repeated Lonnie.

"That's right. You have a beautiful little girl, a redhead like her mama."

"Well, I'll be," Lonnie said, taking a moment for it to soak in. He and Elaine had talked so much about having a son that they really never gave much thought to having a girl. He quickly walked into the cabin and their on the pillow beside Elaine lay the most beautiful baby girl he had ever seen.

"It's a girl, Lonnie," said Elaine, just a hint of anxiety tingeing her voice. "I know you wanted a son, but maybe next time—"

Lonnie's lips cut her words short. "Don't you say one more word, little Mama. She's the purtiest little thing I ever saw. She looks jist like you! Look at that red hair!" Together they laughed and checked the new baby out, counting toes and fingers. Everything was present and accounted for.

"What should we name her, Dearest?" asked Elaine. "We've always talked about having a 'Lonnie Albert Ross, Jr.' but we really never discussed a girl's name."

"Well, now, let's see. A girl's name." Lonnie appeared to be thinking very hard, but after a few moments, he said he came up blank.

"Well, your mother's name was Elizabeth," Elaine said thoughtfully, "and my mother's name is Blanche. What about 'Elizabeth Blanche Ross'?" she suggested.

Lonnie mulled the name over out loud a few times and said with a smile, "I think you've hit a perfect name! That's jist what we'll name her. Elizabeth Blanche Ross," he repeated. Turning to Thelma, he said, "Ma'am, would you mind askin' Buck ta come in here, please?"

Thelma opened the door and Buck jumped up like a jack-in-the-box. "Buck, Lonnie would like fer ya ta come on in," she told him.

Buck walked over to the bed and looked down on a mirror image of Elaine. "Land sakes, alive, gal! That is the purtiest little red head I ever did see!" he exclaimed.

"Elaine, I've got some introductions to make." He stood and put his arm around Buck. "This is my Pa. And, Pa, this is yore family."

Elaine's mouth dropped open and she couldn't say a word for the longest time. Finally she stuttered, "Y-your *Pa*?" She looked at the two of them, standing there grinning from ear to ear. Suddenly it all became crystal clear. The resemblance had always been there, but she just hadn't seen it. How wonderful for her husband to gain a father and a daughter all in one day! "Well, Grandpa, would you like to hold your granddaughter?" she said teasingly. They spent the rest of the day explaining everything to Thelma and Elaine. There was much joy in the Ross household that day!

CHAPTER 22

THE NEXT FIVE YEARS WERE such a blessing for the Ross family. Little Lizzie B. (short for Elizabeth Blanche) grew into an amazing little girl. She never failed to surprise her proud mama and papa with her vivid imagination and her ability to learn new things very quickly. By the time she reached age five, she could already read at a third-grade level and kept her mama on her toes trying to find new things to study to keep her interest.

Lizzie B. stayed a redhead even after she grew out of infancy. Elaine had hoped that her hair would turn blond, brown, or any color but red. She had been teased all her life about being a redhead and had hoped her daughter would be spared that. However, Lonnie loved his two redheads, and when he saw little Lizzie B. running to him, her red curls flying behind her, his heart swelled to almost bursting with love for her.

Twice a month, Elaine and Lizzie B. rode over to the Casey's place where Elaine taught the lessons for all the children and assigned lessons for the next time. Lizzie B. loved the Casey family, every one of them. They were open and funny and noisy—very entertaining for a little girl who was an only child.

Corinne Casey, just three years older than Lizzie B., had become a wonderful friend. Lizzie B was everything Corinne was not: outgoing, extremely smart, and very mature for her age. Corinne loved her little friend dearly. One warm day in September, the children had completed their lessons and were given playtime. This allowed Elaine and Thelma to catch up on their visiting as well.

Lizzie B. and Corinne were taking turns on the swing that Banjo had hung on the big oak tree at the edge of the yard. When they were exhausted with their play, they lay down in the cool grass in the shade. "Lizzie B., what are you gonna do when you grow up?"

Lizzie B. gave some thought to the question and replied, "Well, I think I'd like to be a teacher like Mama. She says one of these days before too long, the settlement will grow big enough that they will need a real school." Another thought hit the precocious child. "Or," she said dramatically, "I might go back to St. Louis where Mama came from and live in the big house with Gramama and Grampapa and teach in a really big school there!" Her big blue eyes sparkled with excitement. She had inherited those eyes from her papa, to her mama's delight.

Lizzie B.'s confidence impressed Corinne. A schoolteacher! How like her smart little friend to want to teach.

"What do you want to do when you grow up?" Lizzie B. asked.

"Well, I guess I'll get married and have kids, like Ma and Pa did," Corrine said contentedly. "Don't you want to get married someday?"

"Maybe, but I don't like boys very much, except your big brother Collin," replied Lizzie B. "Maybe I'll marry him!" The little girls laughed and chewed on grass stems and identified cloud pictures until Elaine called out to say that it was time to go home.

School days were never long enough for Lizzie B. and Corinne, but they knew they'd get to play again in just two weeks. The girls hugged each other, and Lizzie B. climbed onto her little red pony that her Grandpa Buck had given to her on her fifth birthday, and together, she and her mama rode back toward the cabin.

About a half mile from home, Elaine had noticed a nice patch of blackberry bushes. She had brought sacks for her and Lizzie B. to pick some. Lonnie had extracted a promise for a blackberry cobbler from her this morning, and she wanted to pick enough to make some blackberry jelly as well.

Elaine had just commented that Lizzie B. seemed to be getting more berries in her mouth than in her sack. Mother and daughter were laughing gaily, enjoying the warm autumn afternoon. Suddenly, something screamed "*danger*" in Elaine's senses. She didn't know what it was, but fear gripped her and she froze, grabbing Lizzie B. and placing her fingers to her lips. There! She heard it again. Twigs snapped as someone came through the brush toward them. Dropping their berry sacks, Elaine and Lizzie B. sprinted for their mounts, but because they were running so fast, the horses spooked and ran away, leaving them stranded. They began running to the cabin as fast as they could run, still not knowing the source of the danger, but knowing definitely that danger lurked nearby.

They were closer to the cabin now. Just a little farther. Just over the hill, and they would be safe. In horror, Elaine saw a dark cloud of smoke rising up to the sky. As they reached the top of the hill, they looked down on the cabin, already in engulfed in flames. The fences were all knocked down, and her lovely flowers grown from seeds out of Mama's box had been trampled. Poor old Daisy had been killed and lay in the lot just in front of the barn, which was also in flames.

Lonnie. Where are you, Lonnie? Oh, Dear God, please let Lonnie be all right. Her eyes checked the whole place from one side to the other, looking for a sign of who might have done this terrible thing, looking for Lonnie.

There. Lying on the ground out by the garden gate. She started running and screaming, "Lonnie! Lonnie!" dragging Lizzie B. by the hand, her little feet barely touching the ground. As they reached the edge of the yard, she could see Lonnie lying in a pool of blood beside Buck. Neither man moved.

"Oh, dear God, no! Please no!" she cried out, but just as she started to go to them, five Ute braves materialized seemingly out of nowhere. They grabbed Elaine and her precious Lizzie B., threw them onto ponies behind two of the warriors, and rode away. Away from the cabin under the shadow of the Hand of God—away from her beloved Lonnie and away from Grandpa Buck. As they rode away from the only home she had ever known, terror held Lizzie B. in a frozen grip. She couldn't even cry. She knew something was terribly wrong with Papa and Grandpa Buck, and even at her young age, she knew that she would probably never see them again and that their lives would never be the same from this day forward.

Tears streamed down Elaine's face as she recalled that day. She tried to relax and go to sleep, but the pictures from the past wouldn't stop coming. She turned the page in the journal and continued to remember.

CHAPTER 23

Lizzie B. looked at Mama riding behind the big warrior with the scary-looking paint on his face. Mama kept crying and beating the man with her fists. Finally, he pulled up his pony and jumped off. He grabbed Mama and pulled her from the horse. He shook her and she looked like a rag doll. Lizzie B. couldn't hear what they were saying, although she felt pretty sure Mama could understand him. They were looking at her, and the big warrior kept pointing at her. Lizzie B. was a smart little girl, and she knew that the man must be threatening to harm her if Mama didn't cooperate.

Suddenly, Mama looked as though the air had gone out of her. She collapsed on the ground, motionless, no longer crying. The big man climbed onto the horse and yanked Mama up behind him by her arm. They set off again at full gallop.

They traveled hard and fast for a full three days' ride. They were going east. The third evening, they came to a river. The forest was thick and cool. The warriors threw up a makeshift tent for Elaine and Lizzie B. and set about making camp. One of them fished for supper, while a couple of others seemed to be hunting. The other two stayed at camp and watched their prisoners.

The food tasted good after three days of practically nothing but jerky and a few berries. Lizzie B. learned that the big warrior with the painted face was named Two Horse. He seemed to be in charge, and she assumed he was some kind of chief. Elaine had immediately recognized him as the chief who had ordered the torture of Michael Tolbert on the trail. She feared for herself and Lizzie B., but all in all, they were being treated well. So far.

That night, as they lay down, Elaine and Lizzie B. prayed that God would allow them to escape so they could go home. *Home*, thought Elaine. *There is no home to go to. Lonnie and Buck are dead, our house is destroyed. There's nothing to go back to.* She cried herself to sleep.

The morning the raiding party reached the village, cold rain was pelting down. They had been plodding along at their usual pace, when suddenly the Indians began to shout. When she looked up to see what all the shouting was about, she saw it. The village. No wonder her captors were shouting. They were home!

As they drew closer, the people of the village ran out to greet them, women and children laughing and shouting greetings to the returning warriors. The old ones, toothless mouths all smiles, stood aside and watched the families being reunited.

Elaine watched in amazement at the love and affection she saw displayed by the fierce warriors, those who had ripped her from *her* home, toward their own wives and children. She noticed that some seemed to have more than one wife. Buck had told them stories about the polygamous marriages in some of the Indian nations. She had wondered how those relationships could possibly work, given human nature, and how the multiple wives could keep from being jealous of each other.

Elaine stood still, not knowing what they expected of her. An ancient old crone peered at the red hair of the white woman and her child. Suddenly, the old woman grabbed her arm and with surprising strength, practically dragging them through the camp to a small hut; Elaine hung on to Lizzie B. for dear life. Lifting a heavy blanket that served as a door, the old woman shoved them inside. Elaine stumbled and had to do some fancy shuffling to keep from falling on poor Lizzie B., who by this time had begun to cry.

As her eyes became accustomed to the dim light filtering through the smoke hole at the top of the hut, Elaine realized there were others there. She gasped at the number of captives she saw. Women and children crowded the room, both white and Indian from other tribes.

A pretty young white girl who looked to be about seventeen or eighteen asked Elaine in a trembling voice, "Do you know what they're going to do with us?"

They all looked at each other, no one sure of the answer, each one holding imagined horrors in her mind. Then one of the Indian captives spoke up. "Warriors who bring us here will get first choice for wife. Then other men of village get to pick. We are slaves. We must do as we are told, or they will punish us." At the look of horror on the faces of her fellow captives, she continued, "It not so bad. Indian man not like white man. Treat woman with respect as long as she do what he tell her."

The young girl who first spoke broke in, almost in hysterics. "Treat women with respect? How can you possibly believe that anyone who rides miles and miles just to drag us from our homes and families, from everything we hold dear, and bring us to this godforsaken place—how can you say that they treat women with *respect?*" She began to cry, great racking sobs. Elaine went over to her, wrapping her arms around the distraught girl, trying to console her with a confidence she did not feel.

Lizzie B. snuggled up to her mama, great hiccupping sobs engulfing her little body, and Elaine felt totally alone and helpless for the first time in her life.

CHAPTER 24

THE NEXT MORNING, Two Horse sent for Elaine. He told her she would be his woman, his number two wife. She would be allowed to keep Lizzie B. with her. Their names would be changed to Fire Hair and Little Fire Hair. He had only one warning for her. "Do not try to escape," he said. "If you do, I will find you. Squaw line is punishment for trying to run away."

"What is the squaw line?" she asked timidly.

"All women and girls in village make two lines, hold big sticks. Runaway must go from one end of line to other. If you live, you can choose to go free or stay. Most die." Two Horse told Elaine that she and Lizzie B. would continue to stay in the hut. He would summon her when he wished to be with her.

Next morning, Shining Star, wife number one, awakened Elaine roughly. Elaine's presence made her jealous, and she would take every opportunity to make her life as miserable as possible. Shining Star had been assigned to be her guard, teacher, and disciplinarian. She must train her strange white charge with the interesting red hair in the ways and customs of the Ute. The woman spoke halting English. Elaine found the courage to ask her how she had learned it. The answer astonished her. "Utes took me from my white family when I was just a little child," explained Shining Star.

"You're white! Oh, thank God! Maybe we can get back to our families if—"

Shining Star interrupted. "*You* are white. *I* am Ute. Never try to escape. If they catch you, they will kill you. *I* will kill you. Two Horse has chosen you for his number two woman. Listen to my words and learn what I will teach you. He will provide well for you."

"I don't *want* to be his woman!" wailed Elaine. "I'll never let Two Horse near me!"

She received a painful slap to the side of her face. "How can you treat another white woman like this?" sobbed Elaine, unable to take it all in.

Shining Star grabbed her arms and jerked her to her feet, their faces only inches apart. Elaine could smell the foulness of her breath as she said slowly, coldly, "I say this to you only once. I am not white. I am *Ute*. I speak the language to you only because you are *stupid* white woman!" She pushed Elaine back down onto the blanket that served as her bed. "Bring daughter and come!" She stepped out of the hut.

As Elaine and Lizzie B. stepped out of their hut, they looked down the length of the village. Many huts like theirs lined the village, but there were also sod lodges partially in the ground. These were multiple family dwellings, with five or six holes across the top for smoke to escape. In the center of the village stood a large sod lodge, also partially buried. This was the ceremonial lodge, also called the sweat lodge. As chief, Two Horse and his number one family dwelled next to the sweat lodge.

Life in the village was not what Elaine had expected. Torture and mayhem was what all the captives had thought was ahead of them. Instead, they found that in the Ute culture, women are held in a position of respect. They were slaves, but they were treated reasonably well. Elaine had to do backbreaking work, but she didn't mind. It made her so tired that at night, she was asleep almost before she closed her eyes.

Even though it had been several weeks since her capture, Elaine had never become used to the stench of the Indian village. The women were master basket weavers and were able to make baskets that were woven so tightly that they held water. The cooking baskets hung over hot stones where they cooked roots, herbs, berries, and various meats. The cooking baskets were kept going at all times, and the smell made her feel like she could vomit.

She had lice in her hair, and she always felt dirty. Her entire right side, from her shoulder to her fingertips, hurt. They had forced her to grind corn with a hollowed-out stone basin and a round grinding stone.

Her legs stung and itched where she had walked through some stinging nettles down by the creek. Shining Star watched her maliciously, knowing what would happen. When Elaine began to cry out in pain, she laughed as though it were a big joke.

All of that she felt she could stand. However, it was the nights that she dreaded most of all. It didn't happen every night or even every other night, but sometimes, Two Horse would come to her, forcing her to lay with him as his wife. Elaine submitted to him, for she feared for her and Lizzie B.'s life if she did not. She pretended she was dead. Why not? Lonnie was dead. She had nothing to look forward to. If it weren't for Lizzie B., Elaine thought she would kill herself, but she couldn't leave her daughter alone in a bizarre pagan Indian camp with no one to love her or care if she lived or died.

CHAPTER 25

MORNING SKY HAD JET-BLACK BRAIDS down her back; dark brown, almost black, eyes; and a beautiful fawn-colored complexion. Though she was only fourteen years old, she stood taller than most Ute girls her age. It wouldn't be long until she would undergo the womanhood ceremony. She would then be ready for marriage. She would choose the man she would marry, and she already knew the one she wanted. Strong and brave and handsome, he would make a fine husband and be a great warrior someday. Their children would be strong and beautiful.

As she splashed and supervised the smaller children at play in the shallow creek, she observed her adopted sister and the white woman, her mother. Morning Sky liked the white woman and would seek her out at every opportunity. Her sister's strange-sounding English name rolled foreign from her tongue as she said it over and over to herself, "Lizzie B. Lizzie B." She and Lizzie B. had hit if off almost immediately. Morning Sky seemed mesmerized by Lizzie B.'s red curls.

"E-laine," Morning Sky addressed Elaine by her white name, "tell me about the village you came from."

Elaine smiled. She enjoyed telling Morning Sky and Lizzie B. all about growing up in the big city, the big house, the ball gowns, the food, and about Nanny. Morning Sky had never seen a black person, and she was fascinated by Elaine's' description of her.

"Nanny's skin looked coal black, about the color of your hair, and she was bigger around than this!" Elaine made a circle as large as her arms would go. Morning Sky giggled. Black skin? Unbelievable! Fat, she understood!

"Morning Sky, with so many women adopted into the clan, aren't your people afraid that they will just eventually die off, with no one left with the pure blood of the Ute?" Elaine asked.

"That is not possible, E-laine," she answered. "When you were brought into our village, you were adopted into our clan. Your blood is now pure Ute, just as mine is," she said proudly. "Because of wars that have killed many of our people and sickness that the white man has brought into our villages, Sinawaf, The One Above, has declared that the Ute can adopt anyone they choose, and they will become Ute—like you." Elaine realized that the people had allowed themselves to be fooled into this line of thought by the powerful medicine men. She understood that within the foreseeable future, the Utes would be no more because of mixed blood. She understood now. Wars and disease had taken the lives of so many of their tribe that they had begun the practice of stealing women and children from other tribes and sometimes from the white settlers.

Two Horse and Shining Star watched the tableau being played out down at the creek. "Fire Hair and Morning Sky seem to be making friends. This is good. Fire Hair make better wife if she is happy." Shining Star frowned. As the number one wife of Two Horse, she had not relished the idea of him taking on another wife. She had been his only wife for fifteen years. She had born him one child, Morning Sky. Until he captured Elaine, he had never shown any interest in any other squaw. "Fire Hair say to me that Two Horse will never be her husband," Shining Star practically spat the words.

Two Horse snorted and walked off. They both knew he had already taken care of that.

Gradually, Elaine and Lizzie B. settled into a routine. They had quickly learned enough of the language to communicate effectively. Elaine had no idea where they were except that Oregon lay about fourteen days hard ride due west. She had long since given up the idea of even trying to escape for Lizzie B.'s sake. The feisty six-year-old had made friends with the other children. She had become very close to her adopted sister, Morning Sky. Elaine decided that with the exception of the demands of Two Horse, life with the clan wasn't really so bad. Since Lonnie had been killed and their darling cabin burned to the ground, she would just make the best of it. Maybe someday God would see fit to send an angel to rescue them.

She prayed every night for a return to the life she had before, to be able to see her friends and family again. She also prayed every night that, somehow, some way, they would be miraculously rescued. She wished with all her heart to be able to visit the final resting place of her beloved Lonnie.

In the evenings, they would gather with the others in the sweat lodge to listen to storytellers share stories about the People, their way of life, and Sinawaf, The One Above. Songs were sung by those who had been given visions. All this was done to prepare for the annual Bear Dance held each summer. When Lizzie B. asked Morning Sky why they danced the Bear Dance, she told her of two brothers who were hunting in the mountains. One brother saw a bear clawing and dancing around a tree. The bear taught him the song and dance. He told him to teach it to the People as a sign of respect for the bear's spirit, which gives strength.

As the time for the Bear Dance drew near, an air of excitement filled the village. Many preparations were being made for it. The men had to build something called the Bear Dance Corral while the women sewed special clothing for the event.

Members of other clans set up camp nearby, and by the time June rolled around, the valley overflowed with Utes. Finally, the time for the festival came. It had been a long winter, and they were ready to celebrate.

Elaine and Lizzie B. watched as the Bear Dance began. Both men and women participated in the dance. The women's dance was actually almost elegant and very dignified, taking tiny delicate steps—step, stop, step, stop, heads held high. Looking straight ahead, the women held their large feather fans in front of them with one hand, the other hand on her hip. The fringe on their buckskin ceremonial costumes waved back and forth in time to the beat as they swayed and danced to the drums. The men danced more flamboyantly, making aggressive moves with their ceremonial spears and colorful gourds which had been made into rattles.

The dance lasted for four days. They had entered the corral wearing costumes adorned with feathers that signified their worries. At the end of the fourth day, the feathers were hung on a tree at the corral gate, and they would leave their worries behind. Elaine wished she could hang a feather on a tree and she and Lizzie B. could magically be back home. She could hang another, and Lonnie would be alive and well. She allowed herself to cry that day. She didn't cry very often. She didn't want the People to see her as weak.

The best part of the Bear Dance for Elaine and Lizzie B. came when Morning Sky chose her partner for the dance. She had participated in a ceremony with the medicine woman in the sweat lodge. She had asked the spirits to guide her in choosing a partner who would become her husband.

When the drumming began and the dancers started to enter the Bear Dance Corral, Morning Sky walked up to Running Wolf. She held out her hand and smiled. Running Wolf smiled back, and they entered the dance together. Elaine felt happy for them. She knew Morning Sky really cared for Running Wolf and believed him to be the one she should marry.

CHAPTER 26

It would soon be a year since the Utes had destroyed all life as she had known it. Elaine watched with great sadness as Lizzie B. began to forget the life they had known before. They would talk every night before they went to sleep about the cabin, about Papa, and Grandpa Buck. She remembered Corinne Casey and the big swing. She remembered her red pony that Grandpa Buck gave her. Elaine spoke to her of the things of God, but Lizzie B. seemed very confused by it all. She prayed that God would provide a Bible that she could resume teaching Lizzie B. as she had done before.

One day, a drummer came to the village. He had many things for sale, but to Elaine's delight, he had a Bible. She tried to trade him a nice blanket she had woven, but he said no. In the end, she traded him the only thing she had of value—her wedding ring. She also asked him to get word to the Banjo Casey family in the valley below the Hand of God in Oregon that she and her daughter were okay. She prayed he would.

Lizzie B. had forgotten how much she loved to read until Mama bought the Bible. The words came flowing back to her. Suddenly, the things of God that Mama had been telling her started to make sense. No longer were Sinawaf and the one true God mixed up in her mind. Lizzie B. and Elaine held school every day when their work was done. Lizzie B. talked to the other children about the Book and how the Book could talk to you if you knew how to read.

Suddenly, Elaine had a room full of Ute children, all of them excited to learn about the 'Talking Book.' She taught them as she had taught Lizzie B. and the Casey children, and some of them learned very quickly.

One day as she taught the children, Two Horse walked up to them and just stood there, arms folded, listening. It made Elaine very nervous, but she tried not to show it. Without ever saying a word, he left.

She dismissed the children, and she and Lizzie were getting ready for bed when Shining Star entered their hut unceremoniously. "Where is Talking Book?" she asked.

"Why do you want to know?" hedged Elaine, not trusting the woman.

"Two Horse say Talking Book make bad medicine in village. He say get rid of Book," said Shining Star, her eyes glittering with glee at the pain she saw this caused Elaine.

"I won't get rid of it! I will speak to Two Horse and make him understand," said Elaine, and she started for the hut entrance. Shining Star grabbed Lizzie B. and twisted her arm behind her back, causing the child to wince and cry out in pain.

Elaine was on her in an instant. With a clenched fist, she hit the woman squarely in the face, sending her sprawling backward. She had to release Lizzie B. to catch herself. Elaine quickly grabbed Lizzie B. by the shoulders.

"Go find Two Horse. Tell him to come quick!" Elaine told her as she pushed Lizzie B. out of the hut.

Like a cat, Shining Star leapt to her feet, her eyes never leaving Elaine's face. They were circling around, each sizing up the other. "You and your Little Fire Hair have brought nothing but trouble to our village since day you come. I tell you this. I will kill you next time I see you." With these words, she turned to leave the hut, only to run directly into Two Horse who had entered just in time to hear her threat.

"Why do you threaten to kill Fire Hair?" he asked.

"She cause only trouble with her Talking Book!" spat Shining Star jealously. "I will burn book, and things can get back to way they were before she come."

"I cannot allow you to do this thing, Shining Star," responded Two Horse to Elaine's amazement. "Do you not realize that if Ute children learn the words in white man's books that they can know and understand their secrets? Our children can grow up to defend our people against them with their own words! Fire Hair could not give us a better gift. Do you not understand?"

Shining Star spat at Elaine's feet and stormed out of the hut. Two Horse turned back to Elaine. "Fire Hair, this is a good thing you do for children of the Ute. You may continue to teach them from the Talking Book."

"Thank you, my husband," said Elaine, addressing him as she had been instructed, almost gagging on the words. "I will continue to teach the Book."

Two Horse put his hand on her shoulder then turned abruptly and left the hut. Lizzie B. came back in as he was leaving. "Is everything all right, Mama? Can we keep the Bible?"

"Yes, dear, we can keep it. We need to pray and give thanks to God for that wonderful miracle."

"I understand what a miracle is now, Mama. It's something that just couldn't happen, but it happens anyway!" said Lizzie B. in her six-year-old wisdom.

Elaine laughed and hugged her. "That's right, Little Fire Hair! And we'll continue to pray for a miracle that will take us home."

That night, as they knelt and prayed as they had done every night since they'd been there, Lizzie B. prayed with a better understanding in her little heart.

CHAPTER 27

A COLD MORNING SUN PEEKED out over the mountain, revealing the remains of an equally cold campfire. Two figures rolled up in buffalo robes were just beginning to move and stretch as the sunlight filtered through the trees and hit their faces.

The grizzled figure of old Buck Ross stirred the coals in the campfire and threw down the stick with disgust. "Dad-burned sassyfrass wood don't last no time! A feller could freeze ta death! I says last night, I says, 'Lon, we best git some'a that-ere hick-ry wood else we'll plum freeze ta death,' but would he listen? Land, no, he don't listen ta nobody!"

Lonnie, still rolled up in his buffalo robe, smiled a little as he listened to his father's tirade. Buck touched Lonnie on the shoulder a short time later, and they breakfasted on fatback and fried mush. They polished it off with some of Buck's "poisonous" coffee and set about breaking camp.

After they mounted up, Lonnie reached over and clasped Buck's shoulder with a huge, gentle hand. "Buck, there's no sense in you goin' on with me. You have your own life ta lead. You know I appreciate—"

"Now, you lookee here, Lonnie Ross!" Buck broke in. "I reckon as how I kin make up my own mind as ta what I want ta be a-doin' with my time, and I reckon if I choose ta spend it a-chasin' around these here mountains with a crazy man, I kin do that too!" His eyes snapped with indignation. He had missed out on seeing Lonnie grow up, and he had no intention of letting him go now that they had found each other. Seriously, he said, "She's my daughter-in-law, and that's my grandchild. Do ya think I could rest without knowin' if they's alive or dead?"

Tears sprang unbidden into Lonnie's eyes, and a little embarrassed, they clasped hands and rode out of the clearing.

Lonnie knew approximately which direction the Ute village lay, but to be sure, he pulled the crumpled map out of his pocket and consulted it for the hundredth time. It reminded him of the man who had drawn it, and the strange turn of events that led him to the valley below the Hand of God.

After the Ute's stole Elaine and Lizzie B., Lonnie and Buck lay unconscious for several hours, slowly losing their lifeblood from the wounds they suffered trying to protect themselves and keeping the cabin from being destroyed. When Banjo and Thelma found them, they were just barely alive. They took them home, and Thelma nursed them back to health. That, however, had proven to be a very slow process. They were both very badly wounded, and those wounds did not heal overnight.

Lonnie kept trying to get out of bed, pleading with Banjo and Thelma to let him go find Elaine and Lizzie B., but he didn't even have enough strength to swing his legs over the side of the bed.

Buck had something wrong with his eyes. He had a bad head wound, and his vision was very blurry. It scared him a lot, but he tried not to let on. Gradually, his sight started to return, but he would suffer from poor vision for the rest of his life.

One day, a stranger came riding up to the Casey home. "Hello, the house!" he called out respectfully, as one does when visiting a home unexpectedly.

Banjo and all the children came bailing out of the house as usual when there was a visitor. "Hello, stranger!" said Banjo in his friendly manner. "Step down, won't cha? We wuz just preparing' ta set down ta supper if ya'd like ta jine us."

"Well, now that's just the best offer I've had in a while!" said the stranger smiling. "Thankee, I believe I will."

Thelma hospitably added another plate to the table and called the children in to wash up. "There ya are, mister-uh, what did ya say yore name was?" she asked.

"My name's Harry Madsen. I'm a drummer and a trader, mostly with the Injuns, but jist ta anyone who needs what I'm a-sellin'!" he joked.

They laughed politely, but his next words nearly took their breath. "That reminds me of why I'm here. Is this the Casey place?"

Banjo nodded proudly. "Yessirree! It shore is!"

"Well, about three months ago, I was over in Idaho in a Ute village. A captive white woman came up ta me and traded me this fer a Bible. And she asked me ta look you folks up and tell you that she's all right." He handed Thelma Elaine's wedding ring, and she held it up to the lamp. The words "Lonnie and Elaine" were inscribed just as plain as day. "She said her name was Elaine Ross," finished Mr. Madsen.

Thelma grabbed her chest and sat down hard. "Holy God in heaven! Thank You, Jesus!" she said, tears streaming down her face. "I've got to go upstairs and tell Lonnie and Buck."

She repeated the drummer's story and handed Lonnie the wedding band. His face turned white as a sheet, and he started to cry like a baby. "My sweet girls," he sobbed, "they're still alive!" When he regained his composure, he asked Thelma to bring Mr. Madsen upstairs so he might talk to him. He obtained all the information the man knew and verified that the woman he talked to was a redhead, and yes, she had a little redheaded girl with her. Mr. Madsen assured Lonnie that both appeared to be in good health.

At Lonnie's request, he drew a map to the village but said sadly, "You understand, Mr. Ross, that these Injuns migrate around." Mr. Madsen warned,. "They won't necessarily be where they was when I seen 'em."

"Yes, I do understand that. I appreciate ya coming here ta deliver her message. A lotta men in yore position would'a jist fergot about it. I'm much obliged to ya, more'n I can say," said Lonnie, on the verge of tears again.

It was almost another month before Buck and Lonnie were well enough to sit a horse, but as soon as they could, they loaded up their horses and set out for Idaho. Elaine and Lizzie B. had been missing for four months by that time.

CHAPTER 28

Lonnie and Buck followed the trail through the wilderness, limbs slapping them in the face as they rode through the thick forest. Suddenly, Buck said sharply, not completely trusting his eyes. "Look-ee there, Lon! Through them Willer trees over there to the left. Ya see it? It's smoke ain't it, Lon?" He sniffed the air. "I kin smell it! I think we may-a found their camp!"

Lonnie followed Buck's excited instructions, and sure enough, a column of smoke rose from the floor of the valley just over the next hill. Elaine! He couldn't believe that he could be this close to finding her and Lizzie B. Would his daughter even know him anymore? His heart started to pound as they dismounted and slowly crawled up to the edge of the cliff and looked over. The Ute village! The drummer had been right! He looked hard at the village, watching—no, yearning—for a glimpse of red hair, but he couldn't see much in the dimming light.

They decided to wait until full dark to quietly creep down into the valley where they could get a better look. As a bright half-moon rose over the tree tops, the two men eased slowly, oh so slowly, down into the valley toward the village. Suddenly, a rock went hurtling down the hill. They held their breath. Were they discovered? Agonizing minutes went by, but they saw no movement in the sleeping village.

They started down again. Slowly, slowly. They worked their way around to a vantage point that gave them a clear view of the whole village but allowed them to stay completely out of sight. They took turns resting through the remainder of the night, but as the sun began its slow ascent, both men were all eyes, scouring the camp, watching, waiting to catch a glimpse of red hair.

Lonnie stiffened and grabbed Buck's arm. "Look, over there by that last hut!"

Buck's gaze followed Lonnie's pointing finger, and he saw them, two redheads together. One a grown woman, the other a little girl. He felt like whooping and hollering, but instead, he whispered, "Whatcha gonna do now, Lon?"

"We're gonna lay low and watch ta see which hut they go into ta'night. Then we'll see if we cain't sneak down and get 'em outa this place without us all gettin' killed," Lonnie whispered back.

Buck nodded. The plan sounded like a good one.

Shining Star remained furious with Elaine. Before their encounter, she had just ignored the number two wife as much as possible, but now she went out of her way to make things as bad as possible for her. Today was no exception. She walked up to Elaine where she and Lizzie B. were cooking in front of their hut.

She handed her two very large, very heavy baskets and said, "Fire Hair, today you and scrawny child will go up on hill where there are many roots, wild lettuce, and berries. You will not come back until both baskets are full. But if you try to run away, just remember, squaw line will finish you both off." And with a look of pure hatred, she walked away.

Elaine and Lizzie B. looked at the huge baskets then at each other in dismay. They knew it would be next to impossible to fill both baskets in the place Shining Star had directed them to go. They also knew that as slaves they must obey her, so when they had finished their breakfast, they set off up the hill.

They appreciated the peace and quiet away from the hubbub of the village, and they were actually beginning to enjoy themselves as they searched for roots and berries, dropping their finds into the baskets. Stepping behind a big boulder, Lizzie B. shouted, "Mama, come over here! I've found mushrooms!"

As Elaine and Lizzie B. started gathering the mushrooms, they were suddenly grabbed from behind, hands placed over their mouths so they couldn't scream. Elaine desperately tried to free herself. She had to protect Lizzie B.! Then she heard a frantic whisper, "Elaine, stop thrashin' around! It's me, Lonnie!" She stopped dead still, then slowly turned around.

"Lonnie! It *is* you! Oh, thank God! But … but I saw you lying dead in the yard by the cabin. And Buck too," she said looking at Grandpa Buck now holding his granddaughter tight in his arms.

Lonnie pulled her close and held her so tight she could barely breathe. "Naw, as you can see, we wasn't dead, honey. We was just hurt real bad. It took Thelma four months ta git us nursed back to the point we could even set a horse."

"Oh, thank God! Thank God, you're both all right." Elaine held her husband close.

Turning to his daughter, Lonnie held out his arms, and Lizzie B. reached out from Grandpa Buck's clutches and went to her father. "Papa, oh, Papa! I didn't think I'd ever see you again," she cried into his neck.

"And I was afraid you might not even remember me after all this time," said Lonnie, giving her a bear hug, tears streaming down his face.

"Oh, Papa, I could never forget you and Grandpa Buck. Mama and I talked about you all the time."

"Well, come on! We've got ta git you outa here before they realize yore gone," Lonnie said, holding Lizzie B. in one arm and wrapping the other around Elaine.

"Yes, they won't be expecting us back until late this afternoon," she said, looking over her shoulder at the village where she had spent the last year. With an immense sense of relief, she knew her prayers had been answered in a more mighty way than she could have ever imagined!

Elaine held on tight to Lonnie as they rode hard to the west. Lizzie B. rode behind Grandpa Buck. As the sun started down behind the mountains, Lonnie began looking for a safe place to make camp. He chose a small cave, almost invisible from the trail, with great boulders out in front that offered protection from any attack.

Lonnie insisted that Buck rest, and he took the first watch. Elaine and Lizzie B. were exhausted and went to sleep immediately. Lonnie sat on the ground right next to one of the boulders. He had a full view of their surroundings below from his perch. The night sounds were soothing, whip-poor-wills calling to each other and owls hooting off in the distance. Crickets were singing serenely, and try as he might to stay awake, Lonnie's head began to nod.

Lonnie snapped awake. Something was wrong! It was too quiet. He could hear no sound but the wind blowing through the pines. He strained his eyes to see in the darkness. Nothing. Quickly, he ran over and shook Buck awake. "Buck! Git up! I think they're out there!"

Buck needed no other information. He grabbed his rifle and slipped outside the cave with Lonnie. "Did ya see 'em?" he asked.

"Naw, I didn't see anything. I don't know, really, it's just a feelin' I got. It's too quiet out there!" replied Lonnie.

Buck grunted agreement. "Them savages is prob'ly down below us." Both men strained to hear anything out of the ordinary, any sound that would indicate someone walking around down below them, but they heard nothing.

After about an hour, Buck said, putting his arm around Lonnie's shoulders, "Well, maybe yore jist tard, Son. Why don't ya go on in there and lay down, and I'll spell ya out here a while. I'll holler fer sure if'n I hear anything, ya can bet on it!"

Lonnie lay down beside Lizzie B. so that Elaine was on one side of her and he on the other. He gently touched their cheeks and that beautiful red hair. "Thank You, God, fer bringin' my girls back ta me," and with that whispered prayer, he fell instantly asleep.

A gunshot woke him up. He jumped to his feet. Elaine and Lizzie B. were instantly awake, terrified by the shot. "What's the matter, Papa?" asked Lizzie B. in a frightened little voice.

"I don't know, honey, but I'm gonna find out. You stay in here with yore mama and be real quiet, ya hear?" He cupped her chin in his hand, brushed Elaine's lips with his own, and stepped out to the boulder where Buck was keeping watch.

"Where'd that shot come from, Buck?" asked Lonnie in a whisper.

"Right down there by that big tree," he replied. "I couldn't see how many of 'em there is."

After a brief pause, Lonnie said, "Be daylight soon, and you know they'll be all over us."

"Yeah, I know."

Daylight soon began its slow ascent, turning everything from black to gray shadows, then suddenly, the sky became aglow with color. Just as suddenly, Two Horse and his braves launched their attack. Several shots were traded back and forth, then just as suddenly they stopped.

Buck and Lonnie understood. The Utes had the advantage time-wise. All they had to do was sit and wait them out. They just wanted to let them know they were down there. The white men had very little water, very little food. It was only a matter of time until they would have to make a move.

Three days went by. They had given the last of the water to Lizzie B., and the only food they had left was a little hardtack. From below came a voice Elaine recognized immediately. "White Man! Send my woman and her child down to us, and you will live."

"You've got it wrong, Injun!" shouted Lonnie. "She's my woman, and that's my child. Why don't you come on up here and fight like a man and quit hidin' out there in the bushes!"

Two Horse laughed derisively. "You make big talk, White Man. No need to fight. We just wait a few more days, and you all die. You have no water, no food. All we have to do is wait."

Elaine took a good look at the cave where she and Lizzie B. were hiding. As her eyes became accustomed to the darkness, she realized with excitement that she could feel fresh air moving! It was actually blowing their hair as they sat close together. Could there be another way out of here?

Holding Lizzie B. by the hand, she carefully made her way toward the source of the air. She went around a large rock that protruded from the cave wall and gasped. An opening large enough to crawl through! She couldn't believe her eyes. She ran over and looked through. The hill was steep but not impassable. And again God had answered her prayers. There was a spring creating a small pool just outside the opening!

Elaine ran as fast as she could, Lizzie B. right behind her. "Lonnie, come and see what I've found!" she whispered excitedly. "There's an opening in the back of this cave, and there's water out there too!"

Lonnie looked at her in disbelief. "Let's go, Buck. She's found us a way outta this mess!"

Quickly they all ran to the rear of the cave and crawled through the opening. Thirstily, they drank from the cool spring and filled their canteens. It would be a long walk back to Oregon.

As the sun set once again, a voice came from the valley. "White Man!" taunted Two Horse. "There is no reason for woman and child to suffer. Send them down to me, and you can go in peace." No response from the boulder above. "White Man! We have much water here. We have venison to eat." Again, no response from the boulder.

Suspicious now, Two Horse began a slow careful ascent toward the cave. No one tried to stop him; no shots rang out. He reached the cave and saw the bedding on the floor, but the whites were gone. Where did they go? Carefully, he looked into the cave, walking toward the back wall very slowly. He knew these caves could be very treacherous. Fresh air! He reached the protruding rock and looked around. He saw the opening and knew he had lost his prey for the time being.

CHAPTER 29

Lonnie and Buck took turns carrying Lizzie B. on their backs so they could make better time. Buck began to recognize the territory and led them in the direction of a settlement he remembered from his fur trapping days.

They knew Two Horse wouldn't be fooled for very long. They also knew he would figure out how they had escaped and would be in hot pursuit soon. His honor was at stake. White men had breached his camp and stolen his slave wife and her child right out from under his nose.

After two days, they collapsed beside a sparkling stream, covering themselves with pine boughs for safety. They all slept. It was physically impossible for Lonnie or Buck to stay awake one more minute.

Finally rested, they drank their fill and ate some roots and berries that Elaine picked for them. The roots weren't very tasty, but the berries were sweet and the food nourishing. They started their long trek again, this time with Lizzie B. walking. She insisted she could keep up, that she wasn't a baby. And she did keep up! Grandpa Buck told her how proud he was of her.

They had been walking for a week when Buck shouted, "Look-ee, there! Look-ee there! It's the settlement! I tol' you there was a town out here somewhere!" Gratefully, they walked on in to Eagle City. They looked around and spotted a small building that sported a sign saying Hotel. Elaine's eyes lit up. "Oh, Lonnie, could we get a room with a real bed and get a bath?" she asked like a little girl.

"You bet we can," he replied, happy to be able to do something nice for his family after all this time. As he was signing the hotel register, he asked the clerk, "By the way, what territory is this town in?"

"Why, it's Oregon," replied the clerk. They all whooped for joy. The clerk thought they were a strange little group.

They took turns having a nice hot bath then went to a place called Molly's and had a delicious meal. Everyone at Molly's begged them to tell their story and sat spellbound as they did so.

"Ya thank that Injun give up, do ye?" asked an old man eating alone at a table in the corner.

"I don't know," replied Lonnie honestly. "I hope so, but if he ain't, he better watch out."

They stayed in Eagle City for three days and nights, regaining their strength and taking advantage of the safety it afforded them. Finally, they decided it was time to head for the Hand of God and home.

Buck knew the area they now were in like the back of his hand, and he confidently led the little band. They had purchased an old swaybacked plow horse from the man they'd met at Molly's and bought food and blankets at the local trading post. Lizzie B. got to ride all the time, and the adults took turns riding with her.

"How long till we get home, Grandpa Buck?" asked Lizzie B. for the hundredth time.

"Well, it won't be long now. If'n you look right over there"—her gaze followed where he was pointing—"you'll see the Hand of God."

"Mama! The Hand of God is right over there!" shouted Lizzie B. with excitement.

"'Right over there' is farther than you think, Little One," replied Lonnie. "But I'd say we should be in our own front yard in about three days, wouldn't you say, Buck?"

"Yessir, that oughta 'bout do it!"

Sure enough, three days later they walked up to the place where they had once been so happy. The rock chimney stood stark in the deepening twilight, the ashes long gone.

Elaine walked over to the chimney hearth, reaching out to feel the coolness of the stone. There was her teakettle, blackened by the fire, and the cooking hook. She began to cry tearing, gut-wrenching sobs.

Lonnie put his arms around her. "Come on, honey, let's me and you go for a little walk. Want to?" She nodded and leaned her head against him. He looked at Buck over his shoulder, and Buck nodded. He'd keep Lizzie B. occupied while Lonnie and Elaine had some long-awaited time alone.

They walked arm and arm along the river, and they began to talk of the missing time. "I was going to give up, Elaine! If I hadn't found you back there at that camp, I'd made my mind up to just quit looking for you and go back home," Lonnie said with a catch in his voice.

Elaine squeezed his arm and laid her head on his shoulder. "God took care of that though, didn't He?" she asked softly. "I prayed every day that I could find a way to come back home, and everything could be just like before."

After a quiet moment, she asked the question she felt she must ask. "Dearest, you know that much has happened to me since the Utes took me away. You must know that Two Horse had his way with me several times and considered me to be one of his wives." Lonnie stiffened. Elaine began sobbing hysterically. "I knew it! I knew you wouldn't be able to stand to touch me because of all that! Why did I bother to run away? I should have just killed myself! I—!"

Lonnie cut off her tirade with his mouth as he tenderly kissed her again and again.

"Ya've got it all wrong, sweetheart. Yes, I cain't hardly stand ta think of you havin' ta submit yoreself ta that savage, but I know ya didn't have no choice. I don't blame ya fer survivin' any way ya could ta protect Lizzie B. I've never stopped lovin' ya all this time. I've never stopped lookin' and hopin'." His voice broke, and Elaine could see the glint of tears on his face. "We'll teach Lizzie B. how ta act like a little white girl should. And most of all, my sweet girl, we'll forget the past." Lonnie held her close until her sobbing subsided.

"Could you really do that, Lonnie? Could you really forget all about it?" she asked incredulously.

"I fell in love with you when you was still a spoiled little rich girl back in St. Louis. We was as different as daylight and dark, even then," he said with a smile. "For some reason, God allowed us ta be separated for all those months, but it don't matter. We're together now and I still love ya, Elaine. I always will."

Lonnie took her face in those big strong hands of his in the gesture of love she remembered so well. They looked deeply into each other's eyes in the moonlight, and the answers they found there satisfied them both.

Then right there on a soft bed of oak leaves, he convinced her as only a loving husband could. Elaine knew that she was home again at last.

CHAPTER 30

Lonnie, Elaine, and Lizzie B. moved into Buck's cabin with him while they rebuilt their own. Elaine could barely wait to have her own home again.

Thelma Casey had been saving their mail and had a big stack of five whole letters from Ralph and Blanche and two from Amanda (now Amanda Craig, she saw with a smile). She devoured every word over and over again, reading the precious letters until they almost fell apart.

Elaine sat down and wrote a long, long letter to her parents, telling them of the horrors of the past year and a half and how God had wrought a miracle in their lives by bringing their little family together again. She told how Lonnie had found his long-lost father and how precious Grandpa Buck had become to them. And she told them of their beautiful granddaughter, of her wit and bravery, and what a smart little girl she had become.

Elaine and Lizzie B. were busily setting the food on the table as Lonnie and Buck came in. "Well, ladies, how would ya like ta move inta yore own house, say, day after tomorra?" Lonnie asked with a big grin.

"Really, Papa? Day after tomorrow?" asked Lizzie B., clasping her hands in anticipation.

Elaine gave Lonnie a big hug. "Oh, Lonnie, I can't believe it. Our own place again. I can hardly wait!"

"Well, ya won't have ta wait much longer!" chimed in Buck. "Actually, the house itself is purty much done. What we're doin' now is tryin' ta git some furniture put together."

"Oh, Lonnie, can we go look at the house?" cried Elaine.

"Nope, little woman. Not yet. I want ya to see it all completely finished and furnished," replied Lonnie. Then seeing her disappointment, he quickly added, "Just remember, it's only one more day."

"Oh, all right," she said grudgingly. "Day after tomorrow, you said? That's Saturday, right?"

"Right!" both men answered at once. They all laughed and sat down for their meal. They joined hands around the table, and Lonnie voiced the prayer.

"Dear Lord, we're so grateful fer Thy goodness. We thank Thee fer Thy bounty and ask Thee ta bless it this day. Thank Thee, Dear Lord, fer lettin' us be ta'gether as a family agin'. Fergive us our sins. In Thy Name we pray, Amen."

Elaine looked at her husband. She loved him so much and she couldn't believe how he'd grown spiritually these past few months. Before she'd been kidnapped, she had been the one that had prayed aloud. He always said he believed in God, but he just didn't know what to say in a prayer.

When Elaine heard him pray aloud for the first time, they were still on the trail running from Two Horse. His words were eloquent and showed a deep spirituality that she'd not seen in him before. When she asked him about it, he cupped her chin in his hand in the gesture of love she treasured and said, "Honey, when I thought I'd lost ya, at first I blamed God. I thought, 'How could a good God let somethin' awful like that happen ta a sweet woman and a' innocent child?' But as time went by, Thelma and I talked quite a bit while I was laid up over there." He grinned. "You know how persuasive that woman can be. She convinced me that if I ever hoped ta find you two again that I needed ta have Him on my side. She was right," he finished with a kiss on her lips.

Saturday morning, Elaine got up at the crack of dawn, fixing breakfast. She woke everyone up, shouting, "Get up! We're going home today! Get up!"

After breakfast, they loaded up their meager belongings. A little clothing, the blankets, and a frying pan they had purchased in Eagle City, a few pots and pans, and some food that Buck gave them. They would make a trip into Windy Creek as soon as Elaine had a chance to see what all they needed. Lizzie B. was so excited. She could hardly wait to lay eyes on their new cabin.

As they rode up into the yard, Elaine looked at Lonnie and Buck in disbelief. It wasn't a tiny little cabin. It was a real house with a wide front porch with enough room for all four of them to sit on. Lonnie helped her down from the horse and took hold of her hand. Lizzie B. slipped one of her little hands into the other side. Slowly they walked up onto the beautiful new porch. Lonnie reached out, opened the door, and stepped back to allow Elaine and Lizzie B. to enter.

Elaine gasped. "Lonnie! H-how could—where did—what—?" Elaine's voice trailed off. She was speechless.

"Oh, Papa!" said Lizzie B. breathlessly.

Lonnie and Buck were practically dancing; they were so pleased with their surprise. They had worked long and hard, and unbeknownst to Elaine, Banjo Casey and a couple of his boys had been coming over to help them.

"Go ahead, honey," Lonnie said, giving Elaine a little push. She just stood there in one spot, looking around.

The front room ran the full length of the house. It served as the parlor and dining room. Slowly she walked over and peeked into the next room. She squealed with delight. "A real cookstove! Oh, Lonnie, how in the world did you manage to get all this done?"

Lonnie laughed. "I had some help" was all he would say.

The kitchen, though small, was very convenient, boasting a cabinet right next to the stove so she would have lots of work space. All along the wall were lots of shelves for storage. "I love it!" she said over and over again.

Lonnie took her hand and led her from the kitchen and back through the front room to another door. "This is our bedroom," he announced proudly. She saw a beautiful bed and dresser, and in one corner, a rocking chair that looked almost like the one she'd brought from St. Louis. She hugged him with tears in her eyes.

"Now, where's my little Lizzie B.?" he asked as they stepped back into the front room.

"Right here, Papa!" Lizzie B. was quite certain she'd never seen anything so elegant in her whole life.

"Step right over here, young 'un, and climb up that little ladder over there." Lizzie B. did as she was told. "It's a little bedroom, Papa! Is it mine?" she asked incredulously.

"It shore is, Little Bit," piped up Grandpa Buck, who had been watching it all with great delight and satisfaction. "Git on up in there, young 'un, and see whatcha think!"

Lizzie B. climbed the rest of the way into her tiny little loft bedroom and thought how wonderful to have a little space all her very own. "It's a fine room, Papa. Thank you, and you too, Grandpa Buck!"

"Oh, yore welcome, honey," they both replied, beaming.

They worked all that day, cleaning and putting things just where Elaine wanted them. Elaine had been cooking a big pot of beans on her new stove all day, and she made a pan of cornbread to go with them. They ate as though they were starving.

Finally, Buck pushed back from the table. "Whoo-ee! Am I ever full!" he said, patting his stomach. Lizzie B. giggled. "Guess I'll be moseyin' on home. I'll come back over tamarra and help ya build yore corral, son."

"Okay, Buck. I'd be obliged. Yore welcome ta stay all night here if ya'd like, ya know," Lonnie replied.

Buck thanked him kindly but decided to make the short trip back to his own cabin.

The three of them sat close together on the sofa Lonnie and Buck had made, and with Thelma's help, there were comfortable cushions on it in a pretty print.

Lonnie nudged Elaine and nodded toward Lizzie B. They smiled that special smile that all parents smile while watching their children sleep. He picked her up very gently, carried her up the little ladder, and placed her on her very own featherbed. He stood for a moment, just looking at his daughter, thinking how much she looked like her mother, and how very blessed they were to all be together again.

He went back and sat down beside Elaine again. They just sat there in companionable silence, enjoying being able to hold hands and smile at each other. Finally, Elaine said with a yawn, "I believe it's bedtime, Mr. Ross."

With an answering yawn, he said, "I believe yore right, Mrs. Ross."

The time went by swiftly, and slowly the little house became home to them. It seemed to Elaine that Lonnie had been acting rather oddly of late, but when she'd ask him if anything was wrong, he'd just grin and say, "Not a thing!"

They had been in their new house about a month when Thelma had sent Collin over to invite them to the Casey home for Sunday dinner.

Elaine baked a cake and made preparations to go visiting their dear friends. As they drove into the Casey's yard, Elaine noticed a very nice buggy out by the barn. "Looks like the Caseys have invited other company besides us," remarked Elaine. "That's nice, isn't it?"

"Very nice," Lonnie responded, helping her off the wagon.

They knocked on the door, and as usual, out came all the children, grown much bigger now than Lizzie B. remembered, but it didn't take her long to get reacquainted. "Come in, come in!" came Banjo's welcome.

Elaine stepped through the door, holding her cake pan, and she started to ask, "Thelma, where do you want—" but she got no further. There, sitting in the Casey's living room were her mama and papa, Ralph and Blanche Denton! And right beside them were Jessie and Trixie! Lonnie quickly rescued the cake as Elaine cried out with joy and ran to embrace the parents she hadn't seen in almost eight years.

"How did you get here? Why did you make that awful trip, Mama? What—?"

"Whoa! Whoa!" Lonnie broke in. "Give 'em a chance ta answer!"

Blanche Denton held her daughter close, tears streaming down her cheeks. "My dahlin', when we received your letter telling us of your horrible ordeal—the kidnapping—everything, we decided to come. We've missed you more than you could imagine."

Ralph gave Elaine a bear hug. "Oh, Lainey, I didn't think we'd ever get to see you again!" His voice broke.

"We knew we could easily pick up Trixie and Jessie when we came ashore, and that's what we decided to do," said Blanche with a big smile. "We wanted to give you the biggest best surprise we could!"

"Well, I don't think I've ever been more surprised in my whole life," Elaine said, laughing. She stepped back and looked around. Taking Lizzie B.'s hand, she pulled her daughter forward. Proudly she said, "Mama, Papa, I'd like you to meet your granddaughter, Elizabeth Blanche Ross."

Blanche leaned over and placed a delicate hand on each cheek. "You are just the most dahlin' little thing I've ever seen, Elizabeth Blanche Ross," she cooed.

"Mama and Papa call me Lizzie B., ma'am," she said politely.

"You may call me Grandmama and this gentleman is Grandpapa."

Ralph reached down and took her tiny hand in his own. "How do you do, Lizzie B.? It's very nice to be able to finally meet you in person. Your Mama has written letters to us, telling us how pretty you are, but you're even prettier than I expected." Lizzie B colored a bright shade of red. She wasn't used to extravagant compliments, but she definitely liked it.

Elaine turned Lizzie B. around and said, "Trixie and Jessie, this is your niece, Lizzie B. Lizzie B, meet your Aunt Trixie and Uncle Jessie." Lizzie B.'s eyes widened, and she stepped back in fear. She'd never seen a black person before, and she didn't know what to make of big Jessie. He quickly sensed her fear and stooped down. "Little Lizzie B., dat be de finest name Ah bleeves Ah ever heerd a little gal called," he said kindly with a big smile.

Lizzie B. slowly reached out her hand and rubbed Jessie's arm. "Does the black come off?" she asked innocently. Everyone laughed.

"No, honey, dis here is de color Ah is, jist lak white is da color you is," Jessie patiently explained. Lizzie B. visibly relaxed and was soon talking his ear off. About that time, Thelma broke in with "Come on, everybody! Dinner's ready! Let's eat!"

As they ate, they talked and talked. Elaine found out that after her parents had received her letter describing the kidnapping ordeal, they booked passage on a ship and wrote a letter to Trixie and Jessie letting them know of their plans. It took them three months to make the trip, for Blanche said she could not have stood going over land.

Ralph told her he had immediately sent Lonnie a bank draft to cover the expenses of rebuilding and refurnishing the new house. "I wrote him a note and told him not to even think about refusing the money. It was all I could do for my girl and her family in their time of trouble," he said. "I told him we were coming to Oregon." Lonnie had sent a thank-you letter back to him saying how welcome they would be.

"How long can you stay, Mama?" asked Elaine.

"Our return passage is for two months," replied Blanche.

"We've got two whole months! That's wonderful!"

Several days later, Elaine and Blanche were sitting on the sofa in the Ross's front room, with Lizzie B. sitting on the floor. "I have something for you, dahlin,'" said Blanche in that wonderful southern drawl that Lizzie B. had come to love. "You wrote in your letter that everything had been destroyed in the fire. Well, I brought you this." She handed Elaine another cookbook, like the one she had been given for a wedding present.

"Oh, Mama, thank you so much. Someday, I'll give it to Lizzie B. when she grows up and gets married," said Elaine with tears in her eyes.

"And I have one more thing for you." Blanche pulled out a small cedar box. "Here is another blue day box, as I call it," she said. "You wrote how much pleasure it gave you before."

Elaine took the pretty little box, held it down to Lizzie B., and told her to open it. When she lifted the lid, music started to play. Lizzie B. was delighted and played it over and over until finally Elaine had to ask her to stop.

"I'm so glad you came, Mama," Elaine told her mother.

"We knew we almost lost you. We had to make whatever sacrifice it took to get to you, my dear," answered Blanche. They women embraced, knowing their time together was short.

Three more days, and Mama and Papa would have to leave. Elaine couldn't believe the time had passed so quickly. Mama had praised her vegetable garden and her cooking expertise.

The next afternoon, Elaine and Trixie had some time to visit, just the two of them. "Tell me about your home by the sea," said Elaine.

"Oh, the ocean is the biggest, most wonderful thing God ever made!" replied Trixie. "We homesteaded some land right along the coast. Our house sits on a bluff overlooking the water."

Elaine could tell by the look on Trixie's face how much she loved her new home. "And Jessie? How does he like it?"

"Oh, he loves it! There's a big lighthouse just up a ways from us. The watchman came to our house right after we moved in and asked Jessie if he'd like to come to work for him sometimes and help him run the lights. Oh, Elaine, he was so excited! Just like a little boy!" Trixie clasped her hands together in delight as she told of her husband's good fortune.

"Oh, that sounds wonderful!" replied Elaine. "I'm so happy for you, and it has been so good to visit with you these past few weeks."

"I feel the same way," Trixie said. "I hate to leave, and yet I know we must. Jessie has his job and"—she turned and looked around conspiratorially—"I've got my work cut out for me in about five months," she said patting her stomach and smiling.

"No! You're going to have a baby?" Elaine cried, "That's wonderful! Let me know, and maybe Lizzie B. and I can come help you for a while! Would that be okay?"

Trixie took Elaine's hands in hers. "Oh yes, I would *love* it! I don't think my Jessie will be very good at that sort of thing!" The two women laughed gaily and walked back to the house, arm in arm.

Ralph, Lonnie, Jessie, and Buck had spent a lot of time together, and Elaine could tell that her Papa was pretty impressed with the vastness of this wonderful country. She loved the fact that Lonnie and her father seemed to be getting along very well.

They sent Lizzie B. to bed that evening under protest. Ralph and Blanche sat on the sofa with Elaine in the rocking chair and Lonnie and Trixie and Jessie in kitchen chairs. Elaine told the story of her kidnapping and about life in the Ute village. Blanche placed her hand to her chest several times during the telling, but no smelling salts had to be produced.

Lonnie told of their trip on the Oregon Trail, about the torture of Michael Tolbert, and the death of little Colleen Casey.

After the stories were told, they all sat in silence for a long while. Then Ralph said, "Lonnie, I'll be honest with you. I didn't want my little girl marrying you. But she saw something in you that I couldn't see back then. She saw a goodness and a solidness in you, the things that make a real man. And, son, that's what you are, a real man."

Embarrassed by the compliment, Lonnie cleared his throat. "Well, thank ya, kindly sir. That means a lot ta me. I've always felt bad because I knew Elaine's family wasn't exactly happy about our gettin' married. It's real nice ta hear you've changed yore minds."

"I've taken a lot of guff off business associates and people we considered to be our friends when we gave our people their freedom," said Ralph sadly. "But I'd do it all over again because it was the right thing to do." He looked at Trixie and Jessie and smiled. "And I want to thank you for helping me to see slavery in its true light."

Just then, the front door burst open, and Two Horse and a handful of his warriors stood there, weapons in hand. The women screamed. Lonnie jumped up and started toward his rifle standing in the corner by the fireplace, but two of the warriors grabbed him and threw him to the floor. One of them placed the point of a spear against Lonnie's throat and held it there, daring him to move.

"Fire Hair, you come. Where is Little Fire Hair?" asked Two Horse.

"S-she's not here. She stayed with some neighbor children tonight," lied Elaine.

Two Horse grunted. "Come, we go now." He motioned to Trixie and Blanche. "You come too." He grabbed her roughly by the arm and started to drag her toward the door. Two of the other braves grabbed Trixie and Blanche. The women screamed and struggled, trying to break free of their captor's grip.

"Wait a minute!" Ralph Denton's voice had the thunder in it that Elaine remembered so well. "I'll give you money. I have much money. Let me have my wife and daughters back, and I will pay you."

Two Horse stopped in his tracks. Fire Hair was a fine strong woman. He had made great sacrifices to come and find her. But Two Horse was a wise man, and he understood the opportunity that the old white man was offering. He had been hearing about other tribes who were capturing whites and people from other tribes and selling them for ransom. White Man's money could help his clan to buy food and blankets to keep them from the cold this winter. "How much you give?" he asked.

"I'll give you a hundred dollars in gold," offered Ralph.

"Two hundred dollars," said Two Horse.

"Done!" said Ralph. He walked through the bedroom door and pulled out his money belt. Two Horse was right behind him. He grabbed the belt, motioned for his warriors to follow him, and they were gone, just like that.

Blanche fainted for real this time. Elaine and Trixie ran to her, gently rubbing her wrists and patting her cheeks. Slowly, she opened her eyes. "Oh, dear!" was all she could say.

"How much did you have in that belt, sir?" Lonnie asked.

"A thousand dollars, but I don't care. I'd give ten times that much to keep my girls safe," replied Ralph. Lonnie walked over to his father-in-law and shook his hand.

"Thank you, sir. I-I don't know what I would have done if I'd lost 'em agin.'" Lonnie's voice broke.

A little redhead poked out from the loft bedroom above them. "What's all the yelling about?" Lizzie B. asked sleepily. They all looked up at her then at each other then laughed and laughed. Shaking her head at the strange ways of grown-ups, she yawned and went back to bed.

Three days later, the Dentons left to catch their ship. Elaine held them tight, knowing this was most likely the last time she would ever see them.

Lizzie B. cried and cried. "I love you, Grandmama and Grandpapa. I'm so glad I got to meet you."

Blanche stooped down so her face was even with Lizzie B.'s. "We're so very glad we got to meet you too, my dear. Now you be a good little girl and take care of your mama and papa, okay?"

"Yes, ma'am," replied Lizzie B.

"And you will write to us won't you, honey?" asked Ralph.

"Oh, yes, Grandpapa, I will write, I promise."

Jessie picked Lizzie B. up and gave her a big hug. "Uncle Jessie, I'm sorry I tried to rub the black off your arm," she said. Jessie's laughter filled the air. "Dat's all right, honey. No harm done! One a' dese days, maybe you kin talk yo' ma and pa into bringin' you to our place fer a visit. Ah knows a place whur we kin find all kinds of big old seashells. Would ya lak dat?"

"Oh, yes! I would like that a whole lot!" Lizzie B. replied.

There were more hugs and good-byes all around, Then they were gone.

CHAPTER 31

Lizzie B. and Collin Casey were walking arm in arm down by the river. She had turned sixteen this year, and although Collin was eight years older than her, the prophecy she had made to his sister, Corinne, back so many years ago seemed to be coming true. Collin had become a steady caller these days, and he and Lizzie B were very obviously falling in love.

Springtime had come back to the big green valley. The grass in the meadows grew thick and tall. Everywhere, wildflowers bloomed in a cacophony of color. The snowcaps still adorned the mountains.

Lonnie and Elaine sat on the front porch, admiring the flowers that were blooming in the flowerbed from the seeds in the blue day box. "Well, honey, I never have been able ta dress ya in silks and satins. I never have been able ta provide ya with a big mansion." He turned to his wife. "Are ya sorry ya left it all behind?"

She looked him squarely in the eyes and said firmly, "Lonnie Albert Ross! If you ever ask me that again, I'll club you on the head with a frying pan!"

"Yes, ma'am!" he laughed.

"Seriously, Lonnie, I have never regretted one minute, not even one second of my life with you. The only regret I have is the time Two Horse stole from us."

Lonnie pulled her close and cupped her face in his hands. She looked up into those blue eyes—those wonderful blue eyes that drew him to her to begin with—and thought there could be no richer woman in the world!

EPILOGUE

*L*ONNIE IS DEAD. UNBIDDEN, THE words screamed through Elaine's mind. The love of her life was gone forever, and she could do nothing about it. Dawn streaked the dark sky over the Hand of God as Elaine buried her face in her pillow and cried herself to sleep.

About nine o'clock, Lizzie B. pulled up in front of the house and stepped through the screen door, lightly tapping as she did so. "Mama! Are you up?"

Sleepily, Charla rose up from the depths of the sofa. "I guess I must have slept here all night, Grammy!" she said with surprise. "Nanaw told me this wonderful story about when she was a little girl in St. Louis, Missouri!!" Her words came quickly and with excitement.

"And you fell asleep before the end, is that right?" her grandmother said with a smile.

Charla's dimples lit up the room. "I guess I did."

"Is Nanaw still in bed? I can't imagine her sleeping this late." A sudden worry pushed Lizzie B. toward her mother's bedroom. "Mama? Are you awake?" She leaned down and gently touched the old woman's shoulder. Her worst fears were confirmed. Elaine was cold and still.

They laid her to rest beside her beloved Lonnie in the shadow of the distant mountains, the Hand of God looming majestically in the background. Buck had been killed in a hunting accident a few years before, and he also had been laid to rest in the little cemetery bordered by a white picket fence. Lonnie had carved a grave stone with the words: "Here lies John Albert (Buck) Ross. Loving Pa and Grandpa."

Collin planned to make a similar one for Lonnie and Elaine's graves.

After the funeral, the family sat quietly on the front porch that had meant so much to Lonnie and Elaine. They drank in the beauty of the valley below, where the stream was making its way in the shadow of the mountains.

"I can't believe she's gone," whispered Lizzie B. "Both of them gone! It just doesn't seem possible," she said, wiping her eyes.

"I don't think Nanaw wanted to live without Papaw," said Charla with a wisdom beyond her seven years.

"Just remember, they're together again now, honey, for all eternity," replied Lizzie B.

She didn't know just how true her words were, for when Elaine drew her last breath, she found herself crossing that shining river over into heaven. Of all the many streams they had crossed over the years, this was the easiest crossing ever! Swiftly, she went running into Lonnie's waiting arms. They were both young and pain-free again. He swung her up off her feet, then cupped her chin in the gesture of love that she treasured. They embraced long and lovingly. She saw Mama and Papa and little Colleen Casey waiting for them just up the way. And there was her beloved Nanny, smiling and waving!

Lonnie took her hand. "Come. There's Someone I want you to meet," he said.

THE END

ABOUT THE AUTHOR

GLENDA WAS BORN ON A small farm in rural southwest Missouri. After graduating top of her class, she married her high school sweetheart. They remain married after fifty-one years. She has two sons, five grandchildren, and three great-grandchildren. She and her husband still reside on the family farm.

She retired from a career as a board-certified hearing specialist in January of 2016, after being in practice for almost twenty-five years.

Glenda has always been passionate about reading and was greatly influenced in her writing style by such authors as Mark Twain and Louisa Mae Alcott. She admits that writing in dialect was somewhat difficult, but the characters were so real as she developed them that she couldn't write their dialogue any other way.

She is a devout Christian and gives God the glory for giving her the ability to write *And All the Rivers Between*.